Other Titles By Gwyneth Bolton

IF ONLY YOU KNEW

I'M GONNA MAKE YOU LOVE ME

SWEET SENSATION

Divine Destiny

Gwyneth Bolton

Parker Publishing, LLC

Noire Passion is an imprint of Parker Publishing, LLC.

Copyright © 2006 by Gwendolyn Pough

Published by Parker Publishing, LLC
P.O. Box 380-844
Brooklyn, NY 11238
www.parker-publishing.com

ISBN: 1-60043-003-1
ISBN: 978-1-60043-003-9

First Edition

Manufactured in the United States of America

Developmental editing by Chesya Burke, www.chesyaburke.com

Dedication

To the warrior women who paved the way...

This book is dedicated to Audre Lorde for theorizing about the uses of the erotic and the erotic as power, to bell hooks for making us see the revolutionary potential of love, to Octavia Butler, for blazing trails in the world of Science Fiction so fierce that a little black girl like me can come along and feel just fine tapping into the paranormal, and finally to my mother, Donna Pough, who first showed me by example what a true warrior woman is.

Acknowledgements

First and foremost I want to thank God for giving me the talent to write and the desire to share my stories. I want to thank my husband, Cedric Bolton, for always understanding when I have deadlines to meet. I want to thank my mother, Donna Pough, my sisters, Jennifer Pough-Coleman, Cassandra Pough, Michelle Pough, and Tashina Pough. I'd like to thank my nieces, Ashlee Coleman and Zaria Coleman. I love you two so very much. I want to thank my aunts, Helen Hilliard, Diane Crawford, Curlina Glover, and Maxceen Byard and their husbands. Because their long-lasting, loving relationships showed me that black love is indeed black wealth. And I want to thank my Aunt Deloris Reed for always having my back. I want to thank my critique group, The Laptop Dancers, for their encouragement and supportive comments when I came to them with my first attempts at this erotic paranormal romance. Jennifer, Arlene, and Suemarie, you ladies rock! I also want to thank the CNYRW Happy Hundreds. Without the one hundred words a day for one hundred days challenge and listserve, I would have had a hard time making myself make the time to write. Cheryl Johnson thanks for being a supportive friend and confidante. I want to thank the Parker Publishing, LLC family for letting me spread my wings and write this paranormal erotic romance. And thanks to my editor, Chesya Burke, for helping me make it the best it can be.

Prologue

Divine Prophecy
Book of Dana (circa 2050)

The very first people the Divine made and put on earth were all two parts of the same whole. These couples weren't just men and women. Sometimes, the two halves that loved each other and completed one another in ways no other could, shared the same gender. These people were stronger together than they ever could be apart. Most of these original children of the Divine learned to coexist together in harmony. They were long-lived and in their likeness to the Divine shared the power—when they were united—of the Divine herself. The beautiful land she created just for them sat in the middle of a continent so vast and treasure-filled it would continue to be mined for its riches and have them stolen for centuries to come. The Divine gave all this beauty and joy to the first of her children because she wanted nothing but the best for them. All of this made the Divine very happy.

Her brother, the Cultide, couldn't stand for his little sister to have any measure of joy. He'd long since lost their father's favor and been driven from the heavens because his greed and need for power had brought harm to everyone. His resentment made him despise his sister all the more and he wanted to destroy the children she loved so much.

The Cultide caused havoc in the happy garden the Divine created. He managed to make her most favored pairing—the first man and woman union she'd created—find discord with one another. The harmony they shared eked away to nothing once Cultide seeped into their union. He made the man desire to rule his mate in ways the Divine never intended. This desire became sick, twisted, and so restrictive the woman resisted. The unhappiness and lack of harmony the first couple felt became a poison and spread to Divine's other mated pairs. Soon all of the happy unions the Divine created were in trouble. Distrust, hatred, and unhappiness flowed through the land and couldn't be contained. All of this made the Cultide about as happy as one so evil could be.

Divine was greatly troubled. She decided that if her children could not see the great gift they had been given, then they didn't deserve each other. She cast them out of her garden and doomed them to walk the earth apart until they found each other again. Only when her first two children found one another and managed to co-exist, without one trying to rule the other, could the rest of the world truly come to know their Divine mates. So many years passed before the two original children found each other, only to not fully treasure and appreciate one another. Over and over, again and again, they met, resisted their love, gave into it, and sabotaged it with pointless struggles over power and control.

Every lifetime that the Cultide was able to sidetrack them made him stronger and broke the Divine's heart. In what was to be their last chance to get it right, the couple finally saw eye-to-eye and found their way home to each other and the vast continent the Divine created for them. But by this point the Cultide's corruption and evil spread through so much of the world that disease and war reigned. War after war, and new diseases, each one more deadly than the other, began to spread and even though the souls of the original children had finally found one another, they did so too late to save the world.

They were able, in their old age, to find enough people who believed in the power and infinite goodness of the Divine to take refuge underground when the war became so bad all life had been wiped out above. These people and their ancestors would know Divine love in ways similar to the Divine's earlier children. Not all of them would share in Divine power and wisdom. Only the two meant to co-rule would be given a small measure of the Divine so they can put their powers together and spread Divine love.

However, evil never rests. The Cultide remains busy. Even if his little sister rebuilds her haven of happiness, she will do so in a land ravished by bombs and war. He will prevent some people from finding their other halves and true happiness. And he will pull apart those meant to rule together, with only one ruling the other and the land.

When the Divine children finally go above ground again, they will continue to struggle against the evil wrought by the Cultide. Finding love and knowing what to do with it once found is hard. For many years, people walked the earth doomed to a live without their other half. Some were lucky and found their destiny. Other people went to their deaths without knowing the joy such a union could bring. These Divine children will be able to know one another, but they will also be susceptible to the Cultide's trickery. While future generations will have an easier time recognizing the one meant to complete them, people will not always have a mate. Sometimes death and destruction take a life and leaves one mate alone until they have a chance to meet up again. It also doesn't ensure that once people find their mates they'll know what to do with him or her.

When Divine pairings are made, those two will know each other more than any other could and as long as they work together in harmony, they will spread Divine love.

Some of the Divine's new children, those meant to co-rule, will share her power and use it for good. Unfortunately, some will not. Some will let the Cultide rule their power and their spirit while jeopardizing all the Divine has created. While the Cultide won't cease in causing trouble, the chosen children of the Divine should take heart. His wickedness won't rein forever. The Divine won't allow her brother to win. She will send one so strong, so full of power people might mistake this powerful woman-child for the Divine herself. She will restore proper balance to the land and

Chapter 1

Come with me."

Ten-year-old Kara wasn't afraid of the much older and bigger boy trying to make her leave the death-ridden hall with him. Weirdly, she felt connected to him, almost as if she should go with him.

All around her, the people she'd known as friends and elders lay dead. The sweet, sickening smell of blood filled the hot sticky air and made breathing a chore. She knew she should have stayed underground like her mommy told her to. But she thought she might be able to find help. The bad men had hurt her parents; there was so much blood. So she had run through the underground tunnel as fast as her stubby little legs could carry her. When she came above ground, she saw the small homes the people had built with so much love and pride burning down around her. The homes weren't like the huge vacant concrete buildings in the outer bushes, the crumbly buildings from a time long ago before the days of the Divine. Those buildings had withstood bombs and shells of them still stood. The homes in the village weren't built to withstand the fire and destruction engulfing the area.

Some of the people of Ourlane built homes with the rich sturdy woods of the land and some built homes of a mud and grass mixture. They lived on and tilled the land. And now everything was burning to the ground. The crops, the small homes, and the bodies were burning. The red and yellow blazes seemed to lick the purple sky. The only place not yet set ablaze was the town hall.

She ran into the town hall, dodging the bad men and hoping someone would help her get to her mommy and daddy before the men set fire to their home. The only living person in the hall was the boy.

Her parents told her not talk to strangers and definitely never go anywhere with them. The fact that most of the homes in her village were burning, and the majority of the people were dead or dying, made her parents warnings all the more vital. She couldn't go with him.

The outer providences of Ourlane, where they lived, could be dangerous and she'd been schooled early on about safety. Their village wasn't as crime ridden as other villages in the providence. However, sometimes, others came to steal from them because they found a way to survive in spite of the many taxes the monarchy placed on the land. She had heard her father complain about it many times. She couldn't believe she probably wouldn't hear him again.

The boy, who was about twice her size, seemed miffed she wasn't doing exactly what he told her to and he grabbed hold of her arm trying to pull her along. As they touched, a small jolt of electricity went through her.

She wanted to ask him to help her mommy, because she was scared and she just wanted things to be normal again. But she had a feeling he just wanted her to leave and forget all about her parents. She couldn't because their deaths were all her fault. If she hadn't tried to make things better, then the bad men would have never come. She wouldn't ever try to make things better again.

"You have to come with me. It's not safe here and I'm supposed to keep you safe. You have to come back to the castle with me." He yanked her arm. The tall brown boy with deep dark-chocolate eyes seemed to have enormous strength. He also seemed very determined to have his way.

Another shock streamed through her at his touch, and for a minute she really wanted to go with him. This scared even more. She tried to pull away. She couldn't understand why he kept trying to pull her with him, but she knew she had to find a way to get away from him.

"Let me go, please. I have to find help for my mommy." She glanced at him and thought again about seeing if he wanted to help her. He was a lot bigger than her, although not as big as the bad men.

"You have to get out of here. It's too dangerous for us to stay here. Your mother is probably…. You need to come with me now!" His face twisted up in a strange expression and she could tell that he wanted to say something but had decided against it.

He grabbed her hand and started leading her away. Not wanting to go anywhere without her parents, she went wild, kicking and screaming. Her little legs flayed in every direction and several kicks landed on the boy's body. She must have hurt him badly, because he let her go and grabbed a hold of his boy parts. He doubled over in pain and she instantly felt bad. Before she could feel too badly, the boy backhanded her across the face. The force of his strike knocked the wind out of her. She landed on her bottom, hitting the floor with a soft thud. She heaved softly trying to catch her breath and glared at the boy. She had kicked him by mistake; he had struck her on purpose. The thought that he had actually gotten the best of her with his strike angered her. The only thing that made her feel good was watching him grimace and clutch himself in pain.

At first she felt sorry she'd hurt him, but he hurt her too. She swallowed the bitter tasting blood forming behind her lip, and looked into his very angry face. For a moment, she considered pummeling the boy for striking her. She might have been smaller with more baby fat—as her father called it when he squeezed the chubby cheeks on her face—than muscles like the boy, but she thought she might be able to hurt him again if he continued to be mean. He probably wasn't going to be of any help anyway. She'd just have to find a way to help her parents on her own.

Kara only hoped she wasn't too late. She could smell the burning buildings. Thick black and yellow smoke seemed to be trailing into the hall. The burning mud and grass homes made a thick yellow smoke that started to come through the open windows in the hall. Looking at the window, she could see the sky getting dark. The bright red of the sun had dulled to a glowing pink rouge. She didn't want to waste her time struggling with this boy. She needed to find help.

She wondered if the bad men had already burned down her parents little wooden home. Taking her tongue, swirling it, and tasting the blood in her mouth, she tried to think about how to get away from the boy.

Meanwhile, the boy made his recovery and started to move. Once he'd righted himself, he yanked her off the ground and pulled her along. The more he pulled her the more she tried to move away from him, but he held firm.

A voice sounded behind them and she noticed the group of men charging into the hall. "Well, well, well, if it isn't the Crown Prince of Ourlane. Taking to kidnapping have we?"

Uncle Rafe! He could help her mommy and daddy. Kara turned to see her Uncle and smiled in relief. Uncle Rafe gave her a reassuring smile and nodded his head. His dark brown skin glistened with sweat. The black curls on his head had flattened a little with the moisture. He towered above both her and the boy, and she knew he would be able to handle the boy if he had to.

Wearing brown leather chaps and a tunic, Uncle Rafe looked almost scary. Especially since the men with him all wore the same leather clothing along with grim sullen expressions. She'd never seen men wearing the kind of clothing her uncle and his friends wore before. The people in her village wore softer clothes.

She'd heard her father say he needed material that breathed and allowed him to breathe as he worked the land leased to him by the monarchy. It was the only way that he could give the majority of what he'd worked so hard for over to the throne. The more he made, the more the throne took. But he was also able to have a little more to feed his family.

She watched the men as they cleaned up the blood and bodies covering the floor and their faces became masks of hatred. She'd tried *not to look at the bodies. They were her friends, the children she'd played with. The people she'd tried to help. She hadn't been able to help the village, but she might be able to help her uncle and his friends. She almost wished the sadness and anger would go away. She was almost tempted to touch them and try to soothe them. Then she remembered she couldn't.*

The boy didn't let go of her arm, but she was sure her Uncle Rafe would be able to make him see she had to help her parents now. Glancing up at the boy and trying to pull away, she noticed that seeing Uncle Rafe and his friends made the boy hold her tighter.

"You and your men are in treason and it's best that you turn yourselves in so my father might have leniency towards you. You know full well who this young girl is. That's why you and your men destroyed this village." The young boy stood up to the men as if he had an army behind him, which she struggled to understand, since he was a kid just like her.

Uncle Rafe reached out his hand to her as he squinted his eyes a bit. He gave her another nod and she tried to pull away again. She could tell her uncle was becoming increasingly outraged with the young boy because he wouldn't let go of her. She really hoped they wouldn't hurt the boy.

"This young girl is my niece and her destiny is to resist the thieving monarchy and free the land for the people of Ourlane," Rafe narrowed his gaze and spoke his words softly between clenched teeth.

"Her fate is as princess and future Queen—"

Uncle Rafe smacked the boy and snatched Kara's other arm, but the boy wouldn't let go. His face scrunched up angrily but his eyes seemed a little afraid. The boy's hand clutched her arm so tightly, she thought the blood might actually stop flowing.

"Rafe," a young man Kara had never seen before said, "the King's army is all around this place. We need to go. We can't be caught here with the girl. Better we leave the young Prince for now and get away from here."

Uncle Rafe tightened his jaw and nodded for her to try and pull away once more. She did, but the boy held strong. "Let her go now, Prince, and you will live to see another day."

The boy sneered as he clutched her arm. "I cannot. You'll kill her. She's mine."

"She is my niece." Uncle Rafe punched the young boy and yanked Kara so hard something in her arm snapped.

The pain was worse than anything she had ever felt in her life. She could barely focus on what was going on around her because of the piercing, sharp, shooting throb working its way up her arm and through her gut. For a minute, she thought she might throw up— it hurt so bad. She closed her eyes and opened them again and again promising herself she would not cry; she was a big girl now. The boy was on the ground and she saw him lying there just before the pain in her arm became so bad she didn't see anything else.

The Bush 2325 dd

Darwu, the Warrior Prince, woke with a jolt haunted by the same dream from the girl's scared eyes. He hadn't known then how scared she had been. But he had had the next ten years of his life to relive the moment through his dreams. He didn't know why he kept dreaming of her especially since he hadn't been able to save her. He supposed his destiny was to live with the guilt of his failure.

At the time, he was simply trying to save the girl from the uprising. The Resistance had a spy in the castle and had found out that, Kara, the Prince's future sacred mate, would come from that village.

They had planned to destroy the village and kill everyone in it, thus leaving the Prince to a destiny of loneliness. With no heirs to the throne, he would be forced to pick a successor from his cousin's line.

Because he had been only fifteen, he'd been told he couldn't go with the army to save the village. He'd gone anyway, but arrived too late to save anyone…even her.

When he'd discovered her huddled and crying for her mommy in the hall, a small beam of joy had pierced through him. And urgency unlike anything he had ever known made him want to take her with him. He hadn't really understood the wealth of those emotions at fifteen. But living for ten years, knowing she was dead and feeling the darkness seep into his soul, he longed to feel that small beam of joy again, if only for a minute.

He'd tried to rescue her before the Resistance found her, but she'd refused to come. Now she was dead, and he was destined to a bleak mateless existence. A Divine sacred match between true mates was the only way the people of Ourlane would be able to reproduce. He'd heard that a Divine mate offered the perfect connection of mind, body, and spirit. Two halves became a whole and life became better, sweeter.

Darwu didn't know about any of that. He did know that since his mate's death, he'd allowed his own heart to become a hardened shell. The only thing that kept him going was the knowledge he would one day be old enough to make the men who killed her pay. From the time he turned twenty, he'd searched for the rebels to slay them and had yet to find the one who would rather see his own niece dead than serve her rightful role as sacred mate to the prince.

Because of the ongoing battles between the Monarchy and The Resistance, many went mateless—the other part of their soul lost in battle. Darwu hesitated because he knew firsthand the aching emptiness this loss of companionship caused in men. He felt his own soul might be doomed. Avenging her seemed like the only path to some sort of redemption. The only satisfaction in his life was battle, killing the rebel Resistance whenever he found them.

Darwu sat up on his pallet when one of his trusted soldiers, Rohan, came into his quarters. He hoped the men hadn't heard him awaken from the nightmare.

"What is it, Rohan?" Darwu rubbed his eyes, grabbed his leather chaps and slid them on.

"The men have come back from their rounds and they spotted some of the rebels nearby. We must be getting closer to their mainstay." Rohan spoke in a hurried tone and Darwu could tell that the man couldn't wait to battle. The tall, sturdy soldier stood firm, his dark ebony skin offset by gray eyes Darwu always found to be serious and alert.

None of the King's army had ever been this far into the bush. Darwu's father, King Milo, had been content to kill a rebel here and there, whenever one was found trying to recruit members from the villages within the Providence. Only when Darwu became old enough to lead his own group of men against The Resistance did the war became real. Darwu lost count of the casualties on both sides. He wouldn't rest until each of the men who had killed his mate were dead.

He still envisioned the scared little girl, her long dark brown curls pulled back with string, her chubby face masked with determination. He even pictured the torn cotton pants and shirt she'd worn as if she was more content running and climbing trees than sitting and playing with dolls. He could see all of those things, but it became harder and harder to remember her exact features or imagine what she might look like now if she had lived.

Breaking out of his revelry, he glanced at Rohan, "Tomorrow we will go out and search for these rebels. At first daylight, we will hunt them down and we won't stop until we kill them all." As much as he wanted to end the war, a small part of him hesitated. Without the war and his quest for vengeance, what would he have left?

"Wonderful, Your Highness. I have a feeling tomorrow may be the day we bring an end to this. They don't have the weapons we have, and they aren't used to constant fighting like we are. Soon, they will break." A glimmer of pride and happiness exuded from the soldier.

Darwu only hoped Rohan was right. He hadn't come this far to lose to the rebels. He walked with the soldier outside to survey their campsite. The makeshift tents and shacks they'd created as shelter looked weird against the backdrop of barren, broken down cement structures of the long ago city. Darwu had never been so far into the bush, and he scarcely knew why they came to call the ruins the bush when very little plant life thrived there. The inner Providence, the land of gardens the Divine held for her chosen ones, had plants, wildlife, and workable land. The bombed out bush, filled with rubble and tumbled over cement, was the place where rebel resisters hid.

Staring up at the stars in the dark purple night sky, Darwu longed for the hazy purple of daybreak. He couldn't wait to go hunting for the rebels. The Resistance inhabited more of the outer providences. The main core constantly replenished itself and had been impossible to find. But he was determined to defeat them before they influenced more law-abiding citizens' thinking. It angered him that his father hadn't destroyed them years ago when they killed his mate.

"It's quiet tonight. It's never this quiet in the Providence, always something happening." Rohan took a deep breath. "I'd be putting the little ones to bed and spending time with my mate."

Dawru cleared his throat. He'd never really gotten personal with his men. Some of them had mates, but he'd never spoken to them about their mates. Most of what he'd gleaned about being paired he got from watching his parents. The King and Queen of Ourlane were his models for the way couples treated one another. He knew a man's job was to take care of his mate and not only make sure her every need was met, but keep her in line. The King of Ourlane also had the noble task of taking care of the land. Darwu figured he would only have to focus his attention on ruling the land since he had no mate.

Darwu's silence and thoughts about his parents must have caused Rohan some concern.

The soldier laughed nervously and shook his head. "Sorry, Your Highness. It's just nights like this, I miss her so much. I guess that's why I'm eager to get the rebels so we can head back to the civilized world." Rohan smiled sheepishly and appeared as if he was about to walk off.

"So, Rohan, how did you know? How did you know when you'd found your mate? Is it the same for everyone? Is it automatic?" Was the small jolt of joy he'd felt when he touched his lost mate common?

"For me, it was weird. I felt something. But I didn't know what to do with it. It was a powerful need unlike anything I'd ever experienced. But she was the last woman on earth I would have chosen. So I ignored it and thought it would pass. Frankly, my mate had a way of getting on my nerves and I couldn't imagine that the Divine would be so cruel as to send such an insufferable woman to me." Rohan chuckled and stared off into the purple sky.

"So how did you know for sure?" Darwu found himself more interested in the love story than he felt comfortable acknowledging. For one thing, he would never know the connection himself. So it only gave him something to yearn for. Secondly, he was a soldier, a warrior, and he just shouldn't have been so intrigued by such things.

"I couldn't stay away from her. Once I saw her for the first time, she wouldn't leave my thoughts. I had to be with her. So I stopped fighting it and started spending time with her. Not until we made love for the first time did I know for sure. And when my mind melded briefly with hers, I realized I'd found my mate." Rohan smiled at the memory and Darwu began to feel more uncomfortable.

It seemed a bit idiotic to him. He knew if his mate had lived, he would have known her immediately…Silly Rohan, he thought. *Good thing he's better as a soldier than he was at recognizing his love.*

14

Darwu shook his head. He'd heard that sometimes mates didn't automatically recognize each other. Since he'd known his mate the first moment he'd seen her, he knew he wouldn't have been as dense as Rohan.

"Well, I suppose it is a good thing you finally came to your senses. It would have been a waste if you hadn't. Many live their entire lives never knowing the companionship of a sacred mate." Darwu knew women would always be available to him as the crown prince, but he also knew the women meant to satisfy certain baser needs were really no equivalent to a mate.

"Given the times we live in, It's hard to imagine going through life alone. I don't know that I could face the constant war and death without having my family at home. A mate and family, they make it all worthwhile. But they also make me realize how unsafe it is out there. That's why I'm in the army to make sure the law of the land is upheld and to keep the Providence safe for my family." Rohan took a deep breath and Darwu felt a knot in his chest, one of both longing and wonder.

How wonderful to have a larger purpose driving one's actions. All he had keeping him going was the quest for revenge. He wondered what he would do after he defeated The Resistance. He supposed he could work on making things better in the Providence, perhaps even expanding the Providence into the bush and bringing renewed civilization to as much of the land as possible, maybe even the entire continent.

Life on the continent of Khet in the twenty-fourth century was harsh. Legend had it that the advancements made by mankind from nuclear weapons to pollution left much of the rest of the world uninhabitable. The Divine books told that the continent of Khet, once the great continent of Africa and formally Kemet was the origin of the Divine's original chosen people, and after war and devastation took over the world, she decided to go underground until the world above became habitable again. The country of Ourlane and its outer providences were the few remaining spaces on the planet still inhabited by any species. Many of his people believed Ourlane was the location of the Divine's original garden.

The bright and colorful flowers, along with the way the people were able to till and live off of the land, would lead a person to believe the legend was true. Darwu only knew that for some reason the Providence had life and he felt devoted to upholding the ideals of the Providence and the throne. His ancestors had given the people leadership. Ourlane flourished during their leadership and the Divine one who saw fit to spare Ourlane from the fate of the rest of the world granted them sacred mates to ensure their continued rule. He would make sure the Resistance paid for their role in sabotaging what the Divine had decreed.

He'd earned the title of the Warrior Prince because of his ruthless battle tactics. No other prince before him, not even his own father had fought in so many battles and killed so many. They said that because he was doomed to live life without his sacred mate, his heart was turning to stone. He knew his heart already turned to stone when he was fifteen and wasn't strong enough to save her. He lived only for the day when he would come face-to-face with the man who killed her and avenge her death.

Chapter 2

A rush of adrenaline, unlike anything she'd ever experienced, overcame Kara Millan as she noticed how close the king's army was. The army had never ventured this far out into the bush, so The Resistance had always been able to fight and retreat. Darwu, the Warrior Prince, and his bloodthirsty men, were going to make that impossible today.

For years, The Resistance had been able to invade and withdraw from the Providence and go into hiding, recruiting new soldiers and followers very easily. The outrageously high taxes people paid as they struggled to feed themselves and their families had created an open and willing pool of people for The Resistance to convert. Recruiting and training had always been their main duties. After years training for the revolution, they needed to put their training the test. For the past five years, Darwu the Warrior Prince had been on the attack.

Kara found it exhilarating. Her heart ached every time she returned to the bush. The mobile life she led traveling to various campsites had its drawbacks. Seeing children starve because their parents had to decide whether to pay the monarchy's taxes or eat was more than she could tolerate. Watching people toil on the worst land because the monarchy saved the best for their devoted followers—only to give the bulk of what they worked so hard to create back to the corrupt monarchy—caused her blood to boil.

Even as she fought for freedom, she felt she could do more.

The thatched homes where the people lived barely kept the bitter stinging rains of Ourlane off their heads and could have been fortified if only the monarchy considered the peoples' needs instead of its pockets. So, Kara relished knowing that Darwu, the Warrior

Prince, had decided to raise the stakes and conquer The Resistance. If she didn't despise him she might have respected him because he forced them to perform at their full potential. Frankly, all the training and preparation had begun to get a little tedious. Even as she ran with her men, she felt a sense of fulfillment. The time had finally come.

The hollowed concrete buildings abandoned for years, usually made good hiding spaces when they couldn't make it back to The Resistance camp. They'd even made a tunnel underneath the buildings for safe travel back and forth between the bush and the outer Providence. Today she would need to send the majority of her men through the tunnel and keep the Prince and his army at bay for as long as possible. The Resistance couldn't afford to lose the men she had with her.

"Retreat!" Kara called out. A good warrior knew when to retreat and a good leader knew when to save as many men as possible. Kara led them to the sturdiest of the abandoned buildings and directed the majority of them down the stairs. "Head out through the tunnel system and try to make it back to camp."

"But even if we try to retreat, Kara, they will be ahead of us. They have us surrounded. We need to keep fighting. Go out fighting. We can't continue to hide." Cerrill had a point, but one Kara didn't want to hear. The short and stout freedom fighter moved with surprising grace and Kara felt honored to fight alongside him in battle. She respected his insight and knew he felt the same about her.

Everything had been going fine. They had wounded and killed numerous soldiers and then suddenly it seemed the King's entire army was upon them. She had never seen so many of them this far in the bush. She caught a glimpse of the renowned Warrior Prince as she led her men into the area where they were hiding. She'd only seen the images of him on the Ourlane currency, so she wasn't sure it was really him. She felt the same tingling sensation whenever she saw the artistic rendering of him gracing the cina bill.

Something about the profile of his face always made her linger for a moment and she could never figure out why. The same thing happened before she decided to retreat. Her heart fluttered and her mind stalled as if contemplating something. She only hoped the time she spent considering the man who may have been or may not have been the Warrior Prince hadn't cost the Resistance this battle.

If she could get some of the men out of the tunnel safely…but Cerrill was right; they were surrounded by the King's soldiers. Their choices were either fight and be killed or not fight and be killed.

She hadn't considered that being a part of The Resistance one day would mean giving up her life. She also knew she would gladly lay down her life in order for the people to have better lives.

She just felt she had more to give to the cause, almost as if she hadn't done all she could and was destined to do more. But really, what person didn't think they were destined for greater things than they had time in life to accomplish. She couldn't let her delusions of grandeur influence the decisions she made as a warrior. She had no time to ponder such inconsequential things; she had to think about leading her men.

Shaking her head in an effort to clear her thoughts, Kara made the decision to fight. "Well, fine then, Darwu the Warrior Prince," Kara mumbled under her breath. "I would rather die fighting than run and hide."

Biting her lower lip with just the slightest trepidation, Kara tried to keep a hard-edged face as she turned feeling uneasy. How did a routine surveillance check turn into a battle? They didn't usually run into opposition, so they sent one group to survey the land. Kara didn't know why her group had the bad luck of running into the King's army and not her Uncle Rafe or one of the more seasoned leaders, but she knew she had to fight. And in the end, she had to make sure as many as possible lived to fight again.

Oh why can't you just go away, Warrior Prince? These men don't deserve to die. I certainly don't want to die. I'm too young. Someday the monarchy will fall. But if it is not to happen in my lifetime then kill me, Warrior Prince. Kara spoke the words to herself as she prepared to fight the approaching army.

Kara glanced at the men and pictured the mates and children they left at home. People who needed them. Thinking of Cerrill's two small sons and his mate San, who'd already given up a sense of normalcy because of her devotion to the cause, Kara knew that losingCerrill wouldn't be fair. Nothing seemed fair or just. All of the men with her, even the ones without families and mates should have the basic dignity of their lives and they shouldn't have to die while waiting in a building.

She had no one but her uncle. If she had a mate somewhere, hopefully, when their souls met in the great beyond, he would understand her sacrifice. If she had to die, then so be it.

I don't want to die yet, Warrior Prince. But if I have to, then by all that is Divine let it be done already!

Kara closed her eyes to calm and center herself, her decision made. "You all stay back here as long as you can. I will go out and surrender. Maybe I can get away with being a damsel in distress or something." She took a deep breath and exhaled.

"Wait a minute, Kara. Do you hear that?" Cerrill said in a stilted whisper "The King's army appears to be withdrawing . The horses sound as if they are moving away."

Kara listened carefully, her heart nearly bursting out of her chest. They would live to fight again. *Well, thanks a lot Warrior Prince. But one day we will meet in battle. When we do, you better believe I will win.*

"If you don't mind me saying so, Your Highness, I don't really understand. We had them surrounded. We could have taken them out easily. Why didn't we?" Rohan, his second in command spoke in a hushed whisper as they rode away from the spot where they had pushed the rebels into hiding. He clearly didn't want to appear disrespectful by questioning Darwu's decision in front of the other soldiers.

Darwu knew they could have easily destroyed everyone hiding in that broken down deathtrap of a building. On any other day, he wouldn't have thought twice. He wanted nothing more than to see the members of The Resistance dead. But as soon as he was ready to order his men to fire upon the building and defeat the rebels, he felt an odd stirring in his chest. The hair stood up on his neck and his heart actually started to pound abnormally. It didn't appear to be normal battle adrenaline. The only word he could use to describe it is: urgency. He only remembered feeling that kind of urgency once before and experiencing it again in the context of battle made him pull his men back, for now. He knew if he gave the order, he would regret it.

Looking up at the hazy purple sky of Ourlane, Darwu had no idea why he didn't overthrow the rebels. The rebels were clearly desperate and struggling to maintain the fight. He thought he'd even seen a woman with them. The glimpse he caught of her light brown curls as she ran triggered something in him. However, he didn't think he'd spared them because of the woman. As far as he was concerned, a rebel traitor was a rebel traitor no matter their gender. No, he told himself, the woman had absolutely nothing to do with him giving The Resistance a small reprieve. A good warrior knew when to follow his gut and everything in him told him not to kill the small pack of rebels today. As he led his army away from them, he knew he'd made the right decision.

They were further into the bush than any group of soldiers had ever been. The rebel Resistance was growing thin. In time he would see their demise.

"Are you sure, we did the right thing?"

Rafe looked at one of his most stellar comrades, Cerrill, and nodded. If what Cerrill told him was true, they had made the right decision.

"You said the King's army, led by Darwu, the Warrior Prince, had you surrounded and could have killed you all but they retreated. This means one thing. Kara communicated with her mate and she is beginning to come into herself." Rafe really couldn't think of any other reason, as he sat talking with Cerrill just outside of The Resistance's most recent campsite. Most of the others were taking the small reprieve from the constant fighting to rest and communicate telepathically with mates who were still in the Providence or in Resistance safe spaces.

"Can we really be sure, though? I mean most mates aren't able to communicate until an intimate physical connection has been established. Even then full mind merges take a while. I needed several months before I knew the full workings of my mate's mind. And women are not able to get into the heads of their mates until after they have given birth. The two of them have never been intimate. And she hasn't had his child. So how could she have—" Cerrill started.

"If Kara wanted to she could communicate with her mate before any connection had been made. And Darwu—well if prophecy is correct, he doesn't know his own strength. He *still* may not even recognize it, even though we are all but handing it over to him." Rafe paused. Even as he said the words, he felt uneasy about the way they were ensuring that his niece fulfilled her calling. "Kara needs to remember this about herself and the only way that is going to happen is for her to meet her destiny."

Sending her to Darwu and making sure he knew she was coming without telling her about her relation to Darwu, was the equivalent of sending a soldier into battle without proper strategy. The fate of Ourlane rested on Kara remembering her power. They had waited long enough.

"I hope you're right. I felt like a heel leaking the information to Darwu's men. I hope we don't come to regret this." The tired and worn expression on Cerrill's face spoke volumes to the way Rafe felt inside.

"Do you know what you have to do?"

Kara swallowed as she looked at her Uncle Rafe. She didn't want to disappoint him and she had every confidence she could pull it off. She'd trained well with The Resistance and she had no doubts about her fighting skills. Sure, she never thought her uncle would send her to take on the Warrior Prince alone. Although she wouldn't have to fight the Prince, she wasn't sure she would be as successful as her uncle seemed to think she would be at diverting the Prince's attention.

Why would I captivate the rich and powerful Prince? She was no slouch but she'd spent the majority of her life fighting in the outer providences and hiding deep in the bushes and undeveloped portions of Ourlane. Her parents had been killed along with her entire village when she was ten. She didn't remember anything about that experience. The only thing she could clearly envision was the love and kindness she felt from her uncle and the members of The Resistance who'd taken her in. She clearly recalled learning how to fight. From the time she was twelve, they made sure she could properly handle and use the weapons.

Oddly, she'd never really worried about making herself beautiful, even though she was constantly surrounded by strong, virile men, many of them with out a mate, like her. She'd focused all her energy on being the best fighter she could be, which was why she didn't understand how she was supposed to catch the Prince's attention. She doubted that her leather chaps and tunic made for a huge fashion statement. She barely had time to wash her light brown curls, let alone style them in the elaborate braids and twists women in the

Providence wore. Even though the people of Ourlane didn't have many material possessions, most of them made the most of what they owned and managed to look good in the process.

She doubted she would be able to make her appearance suitable enough to make a prince take notice. But, if Uncle Rafe said she could do it, maybe she could. He'd never lied to her before. She took a deep breath. Her uncle had raised her after the king and his army slaughtered her village. She owed him and the Resistance her life and would do whatever she needed to do to aid them.

"I have to distract the prince until Ric and Saunge get there. They'll persuade him to stop his rampant killing of our people and try to get him to convince the king to free the land. But, Uncle Rafe, I really don't see how I am supposed to convince him. I'm sure he has seen a lot of women more beautiful than me. I'm certain he wouldn't be awed by me." Kara wanted to take off into the bush and keep running until she couldn't stop.

Kara thought about the tingling sensation she'd gotten when she caught a glimpse of the prince, the way she felt whenever she saw his face on the cina bill. The man did something to her and she couldn't put her finger on it. She only knew that carrying out this duty would change her life forever. Shrugging slightly and shaking her head, she wrapped her arms around herself and tried to fight off the chill that set in her bones. She glanced up at the dim red sun. Looking at it against the backdrop of the hazy lavender sky, she wondered if she should share her feelings of uneasiness about the prince with her uncle. Would he understand this tingly feeling?

Shaking his head reassuringly, Rafe placed his arm on Kara's shoulder. "Trust me Kara, as soon as he sees you, he won't be able to help himself. Do whatever you need to do to keep him distracted until Ric and Saunge get there. If you can try and get him alone, all the better. He won't suspect you and the troops won't either." His arm slid down her back and he urged her to walk as they talked.

She would do anything for the Resistance, but surely her uncle didn't expect her to sleep with the enemy?

She'd of course had sex before. The brief encounter with one of the younger Resistance comrades hadn't sparked any fire in her. The two quick times they'd managed to be alone long enough to experiment had been a bit awkward. She'd been a virgin and guessed, although he never admitted it, he'd been one too.

The first time, while sweet in a way, ended with him ejaculating minutes after breaking her hymen. The second time, lasted a little longer but still left her unsatisfied. She decided she liked Nic too much to try again and didn't want to give herself a reason to stop speaking to him forever— based solely on the fact that he failed to satisfy her. She cared too much about the rest of her comrades to try and have sex with them.

To her, sex seemed almost pointless without the feelings she saw between sacred mates. The two times she'd had sex had left her feeling empty, which was why she'd decided only to do it again when she met her sacred mate—assuming her mate was even still alive. With so many dead and dying everyday in the ongoing war between the Monarchy and The Resistance, her mate was probably already dead. All the more reason to carry out her uncle's orders she supposed. But still, she had to be sure.

"Alone with him? Uncle, are you saying that I should encourage… that I should let him—"

"I'm saying you should do whatever is necessary to aid The Resistance. You are our only hope to stop the slaughter of our people. Our people only want freedom and to benefit from the land they live, work and die on." Patting her back and offering a boost of confidence, Rafe continued, "The last thing I want is to put you in the same vicinity as that murdering prince, but you are the only one who can divert him long enough. The last thing I want is for him to put his killing hands anywhere near you, but I know without a doubt you are the only one that can get close enough to him. Do it for The Resistance."

His face was grim, and for a slight moment she thought she even saw some hesitation in his eyes. She'd never seen him vacillate before.

It unnerved her so she moved her gaze to the makeshift camp site they'd made for the night. They never stayed in one spot for long and the tents they used, some in bad need of repair, highlighted the Resistance's mobility.

They were deep in the bushes. Past the burned and bombed out buildings, which circled the outer providence—even past the healthier forest. The trees and wildlife in this part of the bush had not fully grown back yet from the war that sent the Divine's chosen underground while the rest of the world suffered and died.

Kara figured the flora and fauna of Ourlane waited for the same freedom from monarchy's oppression the people also wanted. She guessed she had to do whatever she could to help make that happen, even if she had to sacrifice herself to the Warrior Prince.

Rafe watched his niece carefully. He hoped he was doing the right thing. Her destiny and the future of Ourlane depended on Kara being able to make the connections she needed to make.

As she made her way into the bush for a moment of solitude, he debated telling her he'd changed his mind. He wasn't going to send her to the prince, to her sacred mate. But too many lives depended on this union.

"Do you think we're doing the right thing?" Ric, his most trusted man crept up behind him, startling him..

"It's the only thing we can do. It's time. Kara needs to come into her power, confront her destiny, and fulfill it or all is lost." At that moment, Rafe knew he was doing the right thing. While he might not live to see it, the people of Ourlane would know freedom. It was time.

"They plan to use a woman to attack me? What sort of foolishness is this? I have the finest women in the land at my disposal. Who is this woman they hope to tempt me with?"

Astonished, Prince Darwu paced the floor of his makeshift quarters. The roughly built wooden structure kept the rain off his head at night. Between the tables and the wooden benches thrown about the room, it served more as a war strategy room than a place to lay his head. The four walls had become his home away from home even though they were a far cry from the castle where he grew up. Even though the room was his resting spot, only a soft pallet he rarely used in the corner gave any hint anything else happened in here besides plotting and planning.

"Our source didn't know. They were able to give us the plans for ambush, so we will be able to overthrow them if we spilt up the forces," stated Rohan, his right hand and the second in command of the King's army.

Darwu nostrils flared and he waved his hand dismissively. Why was the Resistance sending a whore to do a man's job? For a brief moment he wondered if the woman might be the same woman he'd seen the day before. Not that it would have mattered. Only one woman could get close enough to him to make him vulnerable, and she'd died when she was a child.

Still, the fact that the Resistance would even think to send a woman, must have been a sign they were losing ground. He must be weakening them more than he had anticipated. Maybe he was closer to the day when he could watch Rafe die than he'd thought.

"Leave ten of the men here with me and we will wait for this woman. Tell my men to be on the lookout for her. As soon as they find her encroaching on our campsite, bring her to me. Split the rest of the troops and battle the resisters. Kill as many of them as you can. Take no prisoners. I'm growing tired of this fight."

"Yes, Your Highness. We will do that." Rohan left with speed.

Prince Darwu turned to the pallet in the corner and thought about getting some rest. He was not lying when he told his general he'd grown tired of the battle. He dozed off to sleep thinking of the revenge he would have one day, and hoping his recurring dream would not visit him so that he might get some rest and be ready to handle the latest nuisance of The Resistance.

"Your Highness, we have captured an intruder, sir. A woman." The hulking soldier who held tightly on to her right arm spoke in a clipped military tone. The other big monster, holding her left arm just as unyieldingly, didn't say a word.

Kara struggled to no avail against their brute strength. Somehow, they had known she would be coming. Though she tried to pretend she was just a lost damsel in the woods, they didn't appear to believe her.

The monarchy must have a spy in The Resistance camp. How else would the king's army know exactly where to grab her? She had no way of going back to warn her uncle or the others. She doubted Ric and Saunge would be able to enter the campsite and have a discussion with the prince. The five years of fighting against Darwu and his men had cost many lives. She could almost see why her Uncle Rafe wanted Ric and Saunge to come and try to negotiate a small measure of peace. Even though the task went against every-thing she believed in, she had to fulfill her uncle's wishes.

Maybe she could initiate the conversation and get the prince to see the resisters were tired of the killing and just wanted to negotiate with the throne. Even as she thought about trying to reason with the prince, she knew it would never work. The money hording monarch probably couldn't fathom the concept of reason and objectivity.

She looked into the angry face of the prince and her heart stopped. He was far more gorgeous in person than he looked on his money. Tall and powerfully built, he stood well over six-feet with bulging muscles and cold glaring eyes. His skin was the color of burnt amber and his eyes were a dark chocolate brown. He wore dark leather pants, a male tunic and looked ready for battle.

Strangely, he also seemed to be observing her with more interest than she would have expected. His piercing gaze almost made her feel guilty for coming and trying to talk to him. The way he looked at her made her feel as if she had betrayed him in some horrible way. She could barely stand the accusing glare in his eyes and didn't understand it at all.

She also had to deal with the matter of the fluttering tingling feeling assaulting her senses whenever she saw his image. In front of the large brutally handsome man, the tingles threatened to take over her entire being.

She'd always thought if she saw the Warrior Prince in person she would waste no time cutting his black heart out. Strangely, besides the fact that the men held her and she had no weapon to speak of, she had no desire to cause him harm. Standing before him in the small wooden war room, she wanted to be closer to him.

As his eyes raked over her, she felt a longing just from his gaze. Her breathing stopped and then started again so rapidly she feared she would go into heart failure. Oddly, fear didn't make her heart beat so fast, but a new feeling she never felt before. The feeling caused heat to rise from her neck to her cheeks and a slight dampness in her most intimate spaces.

His heavily muscled chest pulsed in anger and her eyes remained glued to each beat. A scent began to circle the air around her and wafted through her nose. She couldn't describe it because she'd never smelled anything like it before. Daring to glance up into the prince's eyes, she felt her pulse quicken yet again. The connection between the prince, the smell, and her suddenly keening need, collided in her head.

Shaking her head, she tried to clear the overwhelming desire and tingles out of her system. The prince walked around her in circles, making the scent cover her and almost causing her to

29

become dizzy. She thought perhaps the monarchy had created some new weapon.

Then the prince stopped, stood behind her, lifted her hair and pressed his head to her neck. She began to swallow in an almost compulsive manner. Why did the prince smell her? Did he smell the same scent she did? What could it possibly mean?

The prince abruptly pulled away, walked in front of her and stood there.

"So, you're the woman the rebel resisters have sent to try and kill me." The glare in his eyes transferred to his words and she reminded herself he was the enemy despite the sudden tightening of her nipples. The racing of her heart would be a challenge unlike any she'd ever faced.

Tilting her head defiantly, Kara spat out, "What? I'm no killer. You're the murderer, killing people who only want their freedom and the right to the land they toil. I'm here only to try and talk some sense into you so that the killing might end."

The blow across her cheek caught her by surprise. She hadn't expected the prince to strike her. But based on the stories she had heard about the black-hearted Warrior Prince, she shouldn't have been surprised.

She couldn't even lift her arm to wipe the blood from her mouth, because of the two soldiers holding her. Although, she was happy that they were holding her up because the strength of the prince's slap would have undoubtedly knocked her to the ground.

"You will address me with respect and will only speak when given permission to speak. I am Prince Darwu, the Warrior Prince, and you are guilty of treason to the throne. Do you realize the gravity of your crimes?" The prince paced around her as he spoke making several more full circles before stopping in front of her and surveying her with harsh, cold eyes. "Conspiring to kill the prince? Do you realize you can be killed for such an act? The men were sent to ambush me while you distracted me are going to their bloody deaths as we speak."

Letting out a hiss, Kara attempted yet again to correct the prince. "There were only two men coming to talk with you, to get you to see reason—"

The second blow had her on her knees even though the soldiers held her. The soldiers lifted her up. She found that she could barely stand. Though the ringing between her ears was deafening and she could no longer focus her gaze, she didn't want to show weakness.

"Answer me with the respect due your prince." He eyed her and his hand brushed her cheek. After a moment of what felt oddly like a caress, he used his hand to tilt her chin upwards, gazing directly into her eyes.

She could have sworn she saw desire there. Closing her eyes, she tried to pull her sore, aching face away from his hold.

Keeping his firm hold, he commanded. "Open your eyes. What is your name?"

Swallowing, Kara tried her best to build up her resistance. She had no idea what kind of battle technique could help her in this new situation. Nothing in her Resistance training had prepared her for the feelings overcoming her as she dealt with the prince.

His hand maintained its caressing hold. "Your name. Tell me. Now."

"My name is Kara Millan."

The prince removed his hand and moved away from her so quickly one would have thought he'd seen a ghost. His eyes narrowed his lips formed a sneer. "Lies won't help you. Only the truth will help you. What is your real name, wench?"

Not sure why he seemed to get angry when she gave him the information he'd asked for, she huffed, "Kara Millan."

"Your name can't be Kara Millan. Kara Millan died ten years ago." His eyes poured into hers for a second before he shook his head vigorously. "The Resistance did a good job. As I look at you, I can see how they picked you. Perhaps she might have looked a little like you had she lived."

"I don't know what you're talking about. But I am Kara Millan. Maybe the Kara Millan you knew died, but I can assure you I am who I say I am. And as you can see, I'm very much alive." How was she supposed to talk peace to an oaf who couldn't even grasp something as simple as her name? As if she didn't know her own name.

"I'll give you one more chance. What is your name?"

"Ka-ra. Mil-lan."

"Let her go and leave us. Stand guard and kill *anyone* who tries to enter." As he dismissed the men from the room, the prince kept his eyes on her the entire time he spoke.

"Yes, Your Highness." The soldiers spoke in unison, and walked away.

Her knees gave way. The prince caught her before she hit the ground.

She lifted her head as best she could and glared at him. "Why don't you just have them kill me and get it over with?"

"Not yet. By the time I'm through with you, you might very well wish for death, and I may just find it in my heart to grant your wish." His hand caressed her cheek briefly before his eyes narrowed. "But until then, I have other uses for you. You're going to tell me the truth about who you are."

With his arms holding her, she felt electrifying shocks throughout her body. She'd never been so incapacitated with a simple touch. Combined with the dizziness she felt from being struck across the face she found standing difficult.

"You won't get me to tell you anything about The Resistance." She spat the words out and meant them more than she'd ever meant anything in her life. Strangely, she felt she would be able to deny the prince nothing. However, she knew she would never willingly betray The Resistance.

The soothing and seductive scent began to smell like a mixture of pine, clove, cinnamon, and something she could never put into words. But, if pressed, she would have to say desire wafted from the prince right to her nostrils. She desired the prince and she couldn't figure out why. The one reason she could have possibly desired him *couldn't* possibly be. She *refused* to even think it into existence. The Divine couldn't be so cruel. Some new weapon igniting people's senses and making them weak with sexual want must have been developed. Yes, that had to be the answer.

"I don't need you to tell me anything about The Resistance." The prince held her with one arm and used his free hand to gently touch the cheek he'd hit. The soft act sent shivers across every inch of her skin.

He leaned forward and inhaled, taking in her scent. Closing his eyes, he seemed to be savoring her. Before she could process what that could mean, his lips covered hers in a smoldering, passionate kiss. As soon as his mouth touched hers, fire seared her skin scorching her from the outside in. Even though her mind screamed *don't kiss the Warrior Prince*, her body responded immediately. Her mouth opened eagerly and her tongue forged forward aggressively. Her lips pressed onward as if on a mission of destiny. There was almost a marking and a claiming nature to their kissing. She nipped. He licked. She sucked. He bit. Once their hands joined in the exploration, the touching, grabbing and groping took on an almost feverish nature.

Kara's head began to spin and she knew if she kept kissing him, she wouldn't be able to stop. Using what was left of her strength and her sense, she pushed away. Her response to the prince had her unnerved in ways she had never encountered before. She questioned why this was happening, but when these thoughts entered her mind, she quickly silenced them. She didn't even want to think about why she responded to him with the fervor she did.

Taking deep breaths and narrowing his eyes slightly in desire, the prince examined her briefly. His dark eyes held hers and he murmured. "Take off your clothes."

Swallowing and trying without success to pull away, she squeaked. "What?"

Divine Destiny

"Take off your clothing. Now. You still haven't told me the truth about who you are. You'll earn every minute you're allowed to live, and right now you'll earn it by pleasuring me until I'm fully satisfied."

She closed her eyes unable to look at him. She wasn't supposed to want him. "I'd rather die."

The prince caressed her cheek and laughed. "The Resistance sent you here for a reason. They told you to lie to me about who you are for a reason. You will tell me everything before the end of the night. I have ways of making lusty little wenches like you open up. Now you can either tell me what I need to know and spare yourself. Or you can let me get the information from you my way and . . . ." He started to remove her clothing and she stood there in shock. Things were out of hand and she had failed The Resistance.

It was her, the woman he'd glimpsed the other day, the one who had caused—was still causing—the strange reaction in him. A mixture of emotions ran through Prince Darwu's mind as he stripped the clothing from the woman. He'd thought he would simply question her and have her killed along with the other traitors to the throne. But when he saw her, he'd been overwhelmed.

The Resistance had certainly picked the right woman for the job. Even as he looked at her, he had to admire how closely she favored the real Kara Millan. How easy to imagine the little dead girl growing up to be as beautiful as the woman in front of him. The hair was all wrong though. His Kara had had dark brown curls. And he'd often thought the slightly chubby girl would have grown into a more round woman. This woman had some roundness in the right places, but she had a leaner, longer build. They shared the same light brown complexion. But the sweet young girl who was supposed to have been his mate possessed an innocence this rebel wench lacked.

To say he'd been distracted by her would be an understatement, and that fact angered him to no end. The woman had been sent to aid in his assassination and he was attracted to her. Confused, he also felt an intense sense of betrayal just looking in her eyes and knowing she'd been sent to harm him. Why should he feel betrayed by a rebel whore?

Hearing her lies made him strike her, not just once but twice. He'd only struck one other female before and the memories of his action still haunted his dreams. He'd given his share of spankings, some for pleasure and some for punishment, but he'd never struck a woman in the manner that he'd done to the temptress standing in his arms shivering as he removed her clothes. By all that was Divine, she was the most beautiful woman he'd ever seen.

He had to get his emotions under control. By all rights, he really should have just sent her away with his soldiers, let them have their way with her and then kill her. But the thought of any other man touching her upset him even more.

He wanted her. And that was a new feeling for him. The Resistance had picked a woman who could get under his skin as no other ever had and he wanted to know what it was about her that caused such emotion in him. Perhaps she could become his personal whore, since he no longer had a Divine mate. She wouldn't be able to breed, but he would enjoy having her whenever he wanted.

Taking in her long, lean frame, he let his hand caress her skin. Even as he removed the clothing from her body, he knew he would never take her in force. He *would* have her, but she would want it, *desire* it even.

A soft hint of willow, rose, and something he couldn't name wafted around him. The only word that came to mind was seduction, perhaps even desire. But how could he desire a rebel whore?

She was a traitor first and foremost, no matter what attraction he felt.

Once she was completely stripped of clothing, he gazed upon her and his breath stilled. Her body was built for pleasure, *his pleasure*. Perfect tits, a narrow waist, hips, and an ass made for riding strong and long. The soft brown of her skin with hints of red undertones went perfectly with her curly brown hair. He felt he could stare into her light brown eyes forever.

Unnerving, if the traitor in The Resistance camp had not gotten word to them soon enough, the rebel whore would have been able to carry out the plans of The Resistance. He'd fought, waged, and won many battles and he was almost taken down by a wily female. What he couldn't figure out, however, was how. Why was he so intrigued by her?

Slowly pushing her onto the pallet and spreading her legs, he noticed she gasped when his fingers began to probe her tight little sex. He let his thumb massage her clit and brought his mouth down to her nipple.

Her response was addictive. With each climax that rocked through her *he* felt a jolt of energy. He had to taste. Letting his lips trail from her breast down her belly and to her core, he lashed onto her and drank his fill as the orgasms ripped through her. With each sip of her juices he felt more and more in tune with her. Her responses triggered something deep inside of him and he wanted more, had to have more. He let his fingers move inside of her, but he knew that he would never be satisfied with just fingers.

Except for her soft murmuring and stilted staggered breathing, she was silent. He could tell she was confused by her body's response to his maneuverings. He had to remind himself she was still the woman who had been sent by The Resistance to kill him.

Even though he was sure he could continue tasting her until the end of time, he wanted to be inside of her. He stood and caught her gaze as he did. As he undressed, he studied her. His penis was straining against his pants and he was struck with a need so over-powering he couldn't undress fast enough.

He had never known such desire. He wanted to have her, more than that, he wanted to possess her. Her sweet scent still teased his nostrils and beckoned him. Certainly no woman had ever had such an impact on him.

"Who are you? What is your name?" he asked in a voice that sounded like a mix between his own and a wounded animal; he wondered how he even had the presence of mind to form words.

She simply looked at him and then turned away.

Casting the rest of his clothing to the side, he got down on the pallet with her, grabbed her bruised face between his fingers and yanked her head to face him. He had to know who she was, maybe the knowing would give him some clue as to why she had such an effect on him. "Answer me! What is your name?"

"Kara. Kara Millan," she responded in a shaky voice that came out in a half pant.

Prince Darwu shook his head. The lying, bewitching tramp dared to continue and foul the name of his sacred mate. Is that how The Resistance thought they would be able to distract him long enough to kill him? By sending in an imposter to make him believe she was still alive? *How dare they?*

The woman would tell him her real name before they went any further. Trailing kisses down her body he found her core again and started his slow and seductive assault. Just as her legs began to shake with the beginnings of an orgasm, he stopped.

A soft hiss of air escaped her lips and she moaned. Sensing that her breathing had returned to normal, he began to lick and suck and nip at her sex again. Adding his fingers to the mix, he had her panting and on the verge of exploding again. He could tell she was more than ready to consummate the act, but she needed to confess who she really was before he gave her any measure of relief.

"All you have to do is tell me your name and we can both find satisfaction. I'll also see that you get leniency for your treason. A woman such as you probably couldn't help but fall victim to the lying rebels. Tell me your name and I promise to let you find the release you're craving." Darwu idly stroked her soft lean thighs. He wasn't sure he'd be able to hold off much longer. So the woman needed to be honest about who she was, quickly.

"My name is Kara Millan. Now take me or kill me, but end this torture now!" The woman bit her words out between clenched teeth and Darwu's eyes narrowed.

Clearly he would need to find another way to the truth from her. He knew he couldn't hold out much longer and she seemed determined to hold onto her lie.

He used his thigh to spread her legs further apart before thrusting into her, filling her to the hilt. She choked out a sob and he pulled out only to thrust in again. Again and again, harder and harder, over and over, he repeated his actions.

He looked deeply into her eyes. He continued to stare until he connected so deeply that he was inside her mind. He saw her confusion. He saw she wanted to resist everything her body was starting to feel. He saw her trying in vain to fight back the building orgasm. Even more, he saw she wanted to fight her attraction to him, wanted to hate him, but she desired him.

Before he could delve deeper into her mind, to find out exactly why she went along with The Resistance plot on his life, he came to a startling realization just as his climax tore from his loins. With his release, his hold on her mind slipped. Only a small tenuous connection remained, but the fact that they had merged at all let him know who she really was. He would need to bond with her more thoroughly to truly know her.

He knew only of one way he could be in her head so deeply simply through the act of sexual intercourse. He'd heard often enough that the first sexual bond between sacred mates allows the man to see into the woman's mind, heart, and soul. As time went by and the mating bond strengthens, usually after childbirth, the woman was able to mind merge as well. The woman he had just taken truly was his sacred mate.

Kara wasn't totally sure who he was until he entered her, and even then she struggled with her new knowledge. The connection of his sex with hers snapped something inside of her, and she knew without a doubt she belonged with him. Indeed she belonged *to* him. And even though his powerful thrusts were painful and nearly ripped her in half, she found herself needing and desiring more.

His gaze was so intense and looking at him made bits and pieces of her memory come back. She remembered the boy who had tried to take her away from the village before her uncle had shown up. He was that boy. She remembered him saying her fate was as princess and future . . . Uncle Rafe had struck the boy before he could finish. But she could put it all together as she lay silently in the prince's strong arms.

She was the Divine sacred mate of Prince Darwu, the Warrior Prince.

When the prince finally stopped thrusting inside of her, he wrapped her in his arms and pulled her tightly to his chest. Each beat of his heart sent shock waves through her. The scent of clove and desire drawing her to him had mellowed once they mated, but still the scent lingered and she had the feeling it wouldn't take much for it to gain strength and overpower her senses again.

"Do you know who you are?" Even though he whispered the words, his voice was so deep and commanding her heart literally skipped a beat.

She swallowed before she responded. "I am yours." She sighed out the words in a manner expressing the defeat she felt. How could she be the person she was raised to be and also be destined to mate with the prince? Nothing made any sense, but the truth seemed entirely irrefutable. How could she go from warrior to mate in a matter of minutes? How could she go from freedom fighter to being tied to the one man set to destroy everything she believed in?

The prince sat up on the pallet and stared at her intently. She felt as though he could see into her soul. "Did you know who you were when you came here to distract me? Did you allow The Resistance to use your sacred connection to me to aid them in their treasonous assault against the throne?"

She felt him then, in her head and she was startled. She thought she had felt him in her mind when he'd first thrust into her. He could get in her head, apparently at will. She tried to block him. Clearly as new at the connection as she was, Kara had a feeling as Darwu roamed around that he didn't know exactly what to do. Maybe she could use his newness to her advantage. It might have had a chance of working if she weren't so new at their connection.

Wrapping her arms around herself she mumbled, "I didn't know who I was to you. And I was not sent here to help anyone kill you. My uncle told me to distract you until Ric and Saunge came to persuade you to see The Resistance's side and convince you to stop killing them. Your ruthlessness in the face of people who simply wanted their freedom is unconscionable."

"Where is your Uncle Rafe now, Kara?" From the way he asked the question, she knew he simply wanted to see if she would tell him. She would *never* willingly give that information.

Her uncle raised her and she would never betray him. Her uncle led The Resistance, and without him and his steadfast leadership, The Resistance would die. "I don't know where my uncle is." Even as she told the lie, a small part of her ached. Could her connection to the prince prevent her from being untruthful to him?

His hand twisted in her hair and he pulled her head backwards so that she couldn't help but see the angry glare in his eyes.

"Don't lie to me, Kara. You are my mate. You're loyalty is to me. I claim you as mine." The timbre of his voice, so deep and demanding, let her know he meant every word. His voice and the passion in his eyes showed her he meant to possess her.

She didn't bother to struggle. For the first time in her life every warrior sense she had and every fighting instinct was drained from her. Her new fate was totally unexpected and she had no idea how to reconcile her feelings. She knew she would not willingly betray the Resistance, no matter how much her body and her heart made her want to do whatever he said. "I will not betray my uncle! He raised me when the King's army killed my parents, demolished my entire village. I owe him my life."

"Your *uncle* and The Resistance destroyed that village. They destroyed the entire village because they heard that the next royal sacred mate would come from that village. They didn't know who the young girl was, so they killed everyone. I thought they had surely killed you also. I have spent my entire life blaming myself and avenging your death."

He seemed so determined in his statements. Kara sensed that he believed them more than anything. She could also tell he meant what he said about the war he'd waged in her memory. While his declaration showed his devotion for her, it left her feeling cold. That one person had died because of her, sickened her.

"Well, if I am the reason you have been killing all those innocent people, you can stop, since as you can see I'm alive." She couldn't help but cringe at the irony of his words. There would be no more death in her name or because of her; her soul couldn't bear it.

"Those people are not innocent. They are resisters to the throne. They will be brought to justice once and for all." His eyes narrowed and he let go of her hair.

"I will not betray my uncle or my people. They took care of me when I had no family." Slowly she moved away from him on the small pallet.

"They are the reason you have no family. I could very easily retrieve the information from you. With time I will soon be privy to every single one of your thoughts. Such is the way with sacred mates. I would rather you give me the information freely. Tell me where they are." His eyes narrowed slightly, a mixture of warning and desire.

"No!"

He turned her flat on her back then and lifted her arms above her head holding them together with one strong hand while the other probed between her thighs, torturing her slowly as he peered deeply in her eyes. Just as an orgasm wracked her body, he entered her with slow deep thrusts.

Each powerful thrust sent her writhing. She moved her hips to meet his and felt as if she couldn't get enough of him filling her. *Why on earth would that be? And would it ever end?*

She couldn't turn away from him, even though she knew exactly what he was doing. He was in her head, taking all the information she refused to give him.

She tried to hold out, to push him out of her mind, but he was too strong. He easily forged through any shield she threw up. And she had to watch. She couldn't break away from his gaze. In his eyes, she saw hurt and betrayal. His glare revealed his anger, his anger at her.

Why would fate tie her to a man who she'd been taught to hate from the time she could remember? She didn't remember much of her life with her mother and father. But she remembered living with The Resistance and being trained at her uncle's knee to hate the royals and everything they stood for. She knew so many who had died at the hands of Darwu the black-hearted Warrior Prince.

Even though she did not believe she'd been sent to distract him so that he could be killed, the evidence was overwhelming. She was truly the only woman who could.

She also knew that with each stroke of his massive sex he was marking her. Each of his thrusts longer and harder than the last, over and over again, made her aware she would never be able to leave him. She needed him as much as he needed her.

Well at least you're not stupid and you realize the truth of that. Even if you could leave, I would never allow it. As he spoke in her mind, he audibly grunted and buried himself even further in her sex.

She was still very sore from his previous mating, and she was sure even though her body found a strange pleasure in it, she would be in pain later. She had never felt so incredibly full. She realized her other experiment with sex could never have prepared her for her sacred mate. Sex with him filled her mind, body, and spirit.

The sex didn't bother her. It was the mind intrusion that made her most upset. "Do you think it is very warrior-like to use this as a means of getting information?"

If you were not such a stubborn woman, determined to protect your uncle, I wouldn't have to use this. I am tired of this never-ending war with The Resistance, and it will be over, by any means.

He began to thrust his hips forward swiftly and mercilessly. His glare soared deep into her soul as his sex rocked her in the womb. She screamed against her will as an orgasm rocketed through her.

Her head felt as though it would burst. His intrusion was so deft, so all consuming, she let all her defenses fall. She couldn't fight him. She had failed her uncle and The Resistance.

When he finally came with a huge bellow, she was only able to close her eyes in defeat.

Chapter 3

When Kara awoke, she was alone in the prince's quarters. She had no idea where he'd gone, but she had a suspicion he was with his men plotting to take down The Resistance. He knew where they were hiding. She only hoped her uncle had moved the camp. She didn't know if Ric and Saunge made it to the prince's camp or if they were ever coming, or if the prince had told her the truth about their deaths.

So much of what she thought she knew was called into question now. If Darwu was telling the truth, her uncle and the people she had called family for as long as she could remember were responsible for taking her parents' lives.

It couldn't be true. It just couldn't. Yet in her heart she knew Darwu would not lie to her. What did it mean that she had found the other part of her soul in a man she had been taught to despise and he thought she had been sent to kill him?

She couldn't understand why he wouldn't listen to her, why he didn't believe. She would have rather he let his men violate her than to be violated by him. He had no right to take the information from her the way he did.

His rape of her mind was the breaking point. Even though he was not in the room with her, she could still feel him lurking in her mind. That's why she knew she couldn't run away. He'd know the minute she got up to leave and would stop her.

That is right. Go to sleep. You need your rest. He was in her head again.

The fighting spirit slowly coming back to her, she huffed and sat up on the pallet. How unfair! She knew the Divine must have had a reason for making it so that men were able to get into their mates minds from the first moment they connected intimately. But Divine reason hardly stood ground against the sense of intrusion she felt. *Get out of my head.*

Kara, go back to sleep. I'll be back later.

She realized tears were coming down her face too late to do anything about it. Using the palm of her hands, she angrily wiped them away. The Warrior Prince was not going to reduce her to a sniveling idiot. She was in a miserable situation. Any way she looked at it, she was doomed. She couldn't stay with a man who hated her the way he did, who violated her the way he did.

I did not violate you. The first time, you were a prisoner of war and worse things could have happened to you than that. Because I was drawn to you, you were spared that. The second time I claimed you, Kara. You are mine.

His nonchalant, matter-of-fact response did nothing to soothe her mood. Just because he was her mate, just because he had claimed her, did not give him the right to remain in her mind. *You have no right to just stay in my head. You have all the information I have about where The Resistance is located. Get out of my head.*

I cannot. Go to sleep now, Kara, or I will be forced to return. The threat in his words was more than implied.

She was almost tempted to do as she was told; however, she refused to be ruled by him. She would do what she wanted, when she wanted.

I am no longer tired!

Would you like me to help you remedy that?

She wanted to tell him yes and the thought horrified her. She wanted to feel his arms around her. She felt safe with him and the contradiction was too bold for her to grasp. The man violated her mind and thoughts, and yet she felt safe with him and wanted him with her. Surely she must be one sick piece of work.

No, she lied. *I do not need you to help me remedy anything. Stay there and continue with your plot to kill the innocent.*

I will soon teach you not to lie to me, Kara.

If you are in my head and know my thoughts, why ask me questions? You know the answers. Leave me alone. Or better yet get out of my head. His constant questioning while he moved freely about her most private thoughts and memories made her want to scream.

The door opened with a burst. It hit the semi sturdy wall of the quarters so hard the makeshift building shifted slightly. If she hadn't been so irritated already, she might have taken a moment to be a little concerned.

Clearly you can walk and pick brains at the same time, she thought wryly.

"Get up, Kara. Come to me."

She lifted her head from the pallet and saw him standing in the doorway.

When she didn't immediately get up and come to him, he repeated himself. Kara turned away from him and faced the wall. She decided that even though the prince was her sacred mate and she was linked to him in ways she did not fully understand or want to understand, she was not going to become his puppet. The rest of the Ourlane might jump when he snapped, but she would not.

He walked over to the pallet, reached down and pulled her up. She struggled unsuccessfully to free herself from his grip and when that failed she attempted to knee him in the groin.

He caught her knee before it made contact and glowered at her. "Have you lost your mind?"

"No, I just have an unwanted guest there. Unless you leave my head, I can promise you will see just how crazy and destructive I can be."

His eyes narrowed and he spoke between clenched teeth. "You should know, Kara, I expect obedience not only from the subjects of Ourlane, but most especially from you, my sacred mate. If you continue to behave in this manner, I will have no choice but to punish you."

She tilted her head defiantly. "I'd gladly take punishment rather than be tied to you and have you in my head. You had no right to violate me in this way. I want to leave."

"Do you realize the only reason you are still alive is because of who you are? You should be thanking the Divine you are my sacred mate and I can read your every thought, know your every need, and fulfill your every desire. If that were not the case, you would be killed for treason." He spat out the words and shook her.

Cringing at his words, Kara's mind and heart immediately went to The Resistance and their fate. "Do you plan to do kill my uncle and the others? Kill them because they happen to believe in self-fulfillment and not lacing the pockets of the overly rich and overly pampered royal family?"

If Darwu were truly her Divine mate, she should be able to get him to see that the people of Ourlane deserved better, than living in barely inhabitable homes and giving more of their resources than should be allowed to pay outrageous taxes to the monarchy. If he were the one meant to complete her, he should be able to see that The Resistance's cause—to free the people and free the land—was a noble one, not something to be killed for but to be commended.

"Kara, don't defend those traitors to the throne. They're in violation to the order of this land and they must be dealt with." Speaking through clenched teeth, she saw that the Prince's patience had worn thin.

"Do not kill my uncle," she pleaded. He had to understand. She didn't want her uncle to die because she had failed.

"Your uncle is the ringleader, Kara. He must be punished. I suggest you not worry yourself with this." A dismissive glance was all he gave her as he pronounced the fate of the people she loved.

Angered, she struggled to pull away again. If he wasn't going to even try and see things her way then they were doomed. She might as well be dead than live with a mate who didn't try to understand her. She refused to stand by while the people of Ourlane continued to recycle rags of clothing and till the land just to lace the pockets of the ruling class. "They are my people. I refuse to live if they are to die. I want to be punished with them."

The expression on Darwu's darkly masked face twisted and a shadow covered his eyes. He took several deep, halting breaths, as if trying to calm himself. "That is not up to you to decide."

"I admit I came here to kill you and I will if you kill my uncle and the others. So you should take care of me with them." She'd rather die with The Resistance than live knowing her actions and her destiny had betrayed them.

His gaze narrowed in on her. "You forget I have been in your head. I know everything there is to know about you, Kara. I even see the lies you tell right now for what they are. And while some might find your loyalty to your uncle and The Resistance admirable, I find it detestable. If you continue to provoke me, I will be forced to punish you until you see the error of your ways. Am I clear?"

She frowned and tried to turn away. He yanked her and made sure she continued to face his menacing glare. She let out an angry hiss and squirmed to release herself.

"Am I clear, Kara?" His lips curled into an almost snarl as he spoke.

A lesser woman might have had the common sense to be afraid. Kara found herself becoming increasingly annoyed. Did he really think he could just boss her around and bend her to his will by giving her angry glares and harsh words? If so, someone should tell the Warrior Prince he had the wrong woman. She refused to be cowed by him or anyone else.

She pursed her lips and rolled her eyes. If he wanted to be a stubborn arrogant beast, she figured they could have a test of wills. "Shouldn't you be out killing innocent people? Why are you still here bothering me?"

"Fine, you were warned." He started to walk over to a bench in the corner of the room and pulled her with him. She struggled to no avail and when he reached the bench he sat and draped her struggling naked body over his knees.

As soon as the reality of what was about to happen set in, the first swat landed on her backside, not so gently.

His hand landed swiftly and repeatedly, each strike harder than the last and landing on various parts of her buttocks and thighs. She squirmed and wiggled trying to break away from his stinging hands. Each move triggered her traitorous nipples and clit until she swore she might actually climax from the horrible act. She willed her dignity not to fail her even as she held back a moan.

"Now, Kara, I want you to tell me if you understand me yet?" *Whap. Whap.* "Or, will I have to continue punishing you in this manner until you're clear?"

Kara couldn't muster the strength to form words. The horror of being spanked like a misbehaving child was too much to bear. Beyond embarrassed and ashamed, she could only sob softly and hope the prince would tire of spanking her soon.

"Kara, I need you to answer me. You will not bring up your uncle and the other traitors again and you will not attempt to plead their case to me or anyone else." *Whap. Whap. Whap.* "They are traitors and will be punished accordingly. You are my sacred mate, and you will show me the proper respect and obey me in all I say. Is that clear?"

"Y-y-y-es. It's c-c-clear. Please, p-please stop." Kara gritted her teeth against the impending orgasm threatening to rip through her body. She refused to come from a spanking.

His hand landed several more times before he stopped and stood her upright.

With her butt on fire, and tears streaming down her face, she couldn't believe she was so aroused. The prince stood, his hand still holding her. He bent his head and began to kiss away the tears from her face.

Picking her up, he took her back to the pallet. He laid her down and began to disrobe. She allowed her eyes to take in the strong muscled length of him. Every inch of his body signaled perfection. She mused that if she had ever ran into him on the battlefield or in the bush she might have been hard pressed trying to decide what to do with him. Soaking in the smooth, dark brown skin, which covered the bulges of steel caused her mouth to fall open. *Divine help me.* She wanted him more than anything. And given how much she also wanted freedom for the people of Ourlane, that want no doubt caused her nothing but conflict and confusion.

The Warrior Prince was certainly a sight to behold. His dark skin rippled with muscular strength. His piercing obsidian eyes seared with seduction. And he was all hers. He might have taken solace in claiming her. But she knew that despite the way men chose to understand the Divine sacred connection, it worked both ways. They belonged to one another.

The sensations trailing over her body after his punishment had her sopping wet and writhing with need. She did not understand why. In the short amount of time she had been with Darwu, she had experienced more passion and emotion than she ever thought possible. She knew they had just tapped the surface of intensity they could reach. Would she be able to take more?

The scent came back full force, seeping in through her nostrils and assaulting her body as well as her brain. From that day forward, if anyone asked her if desire had a scent she would respond yes and its name was Darwu.

Darwu removed his leather chaps and tunic and stood before her naked. The muscles that rippled his chest and bulked from his arms and powerful thighs made her breathless. The hardened protrusion of his penis made her mouth water. She had a sudden desire to taste him.

Not tonight, Love. But once your luscious lips heal I will have you take me that way. He got down on the pallet and turned her over onto her stomach. *I want to look at your beautifully marked bottom when I take you.* He lifted her to her hands and knees and thrust into her from behind.

The feel of his muscular thighs on her sore bottom sent the sensations tingling across her entire body. He filled her so completely she felt as if she were about to burst. His hands grabbed her ass roughly and the touch caused more shock waves to her already heated behind.

"Oh!" a climax ripped through her and she thought she would surely die. She had never felt anything so intense.

Darwu worked his hips feverishly thrusting, in and out, harder and faster, deeper and longer. Each thrust sent her spiraling, as if he had the ability to send her into orbit.

You are mine, Kara Millan. Mine. All mine. He spoke directly into her mind. Even his grunts and moans were in her head. The combination of him in her mind along with the incredible strokes of his strong and satisfying sex had her trembling. She didn't need him to tell her she was his. She needed the Divine, someone, anyone, to tell her what she was supposed to do about it.

How was she supposed to reconcile the tidal wave of conflicted feelings the prince and her devotions to the cause of her people aroused in her? How was it possible that she wanted to cry out in mind shocking, body rocking pleasure at the same time she wanted to cry out against the dying freedom movement of The Resistance?

"If you insist on harboring thoughts about the treasonous Resistance, I have no choice but to mark this round frame." The flat of Darwu's hands snapped her out of her musing about the fate of The Resistance.

The punishing palm found a nice rhythm with his penis. Each stroke in lunged her forward with a slap on her butt cheek. Each withdrawal left her whimpering as he caressed the offended cheek, penetrated again and offered another slap to the neglected cheek. The smarting of her ass and the pulsing of her core, combined with the sultry friction of his penis, became altogether too much for her to handle.

He must have sensed she was about to explode. She heard him chuckling inside her head. *If this is what I need to do to remove all thoughts of those traitors from your mind then I will gladly do so. I will gladly take you until the only thoughts in your mind are of me.*

Me. Darwu, the Warrior Prince. Your. Divine. Sacred. Mate. You belong to me!

The bellow that came after that declaration sent her over the top and she screamed out her orgasm as she thrust her hips back to take him deeper. As her sex clutched his, she felt him explode inside of her and she felt herself feverishly milking him, draining him, and wanting more. She collapsed onto the pallet and he fell on top of her. He rolled over and caressed her with his powerful hands.

Darwu held her for some time, soothing her with his hands, paying homage to her body with soft subtle brushes of his lips.

She tried not to think about why she didn't want him to let her go. Everything that had happened to her from the moment she set foot on the campsite had her head spinning and her mind swimming with confusion.

Darwu gave her one more seductive squeeze before sitting up on the pallet. *I am going to leave you so that you can rest, Kara. Do not ask me to leave your head. I can't. We are bonded. You are my mate. I can't be disconnected from you. Sleep, Love.*

She watched him rise and put on his clothing, closing her eyes as he walked out of the quarters.

Chapter 4

Darwu finally had the leaders of The Resistance in custody. His men found Kara's uncle and his unsuspecting followers exactly where he'd calculated they'd be.

He'd hated getting information from her that way, especially when he saw the violated look in her eyes. But he had to get the traitors. As much as she lamented the fate of the people of Ourlane, Darwu didn't understand why his mate couldn't see that The Resistance threatened the natural order. They threatened everything that delivered structure and peace. So the people weren't all living in luxury. They weren't all meant to. Everyone couldn't be rich. And everyone had their place in society. His family had been chosen to rule. Now he would have heirs since he found his mate, but The Resistance threatened their legacy.

Having found his sacred mate made *everything* different. He'd no longer be able to spend long periods of time in the outer providences and in the bush searching for The Resistance. He wouldn't be able to stay away from her that long. Strangely, he found it hard to be away from her for even a few minutes. He supposed that was why the Divine allowed mates to share thoughts telepathically.

Being inside her head intrigued him. He still hadn't figured out the full workings of her mind. But he didn't think it would take him long to do so. Where some mates may have taken months, indeed years to fully connect, he knew he needed to quickly enter his mate's mind. The sooner he mastered her and destroyed the rebels, the better things would be for all.

He needed to wipe out the remnants of Rafe's camp once and for all. Then he would be able to take his woman back to the castle and start making future heirs.

Divine Destiny

He'd found his mate. The woman who'd haunted him ever since he was fifteen. She'd always been alive. If he could not read her every thought and did not know she really hadn't come to the camp to kill him, he would have thought that it was too good to be true.

As it was, he still didn't fully trust her. She lied. She defended The Resistance. She would rather be killed with them than to live out her destiny with him. She was the future Queen of Ourlane and she wanted to die with a bunch of traitors who had given the throne nothing but trouble for as long as he could remember.

He was irritated because she couldn't see that her uncle and his followers weren't the trustworthy warriors she thought them to be. Her continuing to believe in their cause, even after he'd claimed her as his own, angered him. The sense of betrayal he felt when she first walked into his quarters threatened to grow and multiply now that he knew who she really was.

He hadn't wanted to punish her but she refused to obey and her disobedience was something he could not tolerate. She had to learn her place and learn it quickly. Again, he thought of his own parents. The queen could be a spirited and opinionated woman, and Darwu was sure his father often found that entertaining. However, when it came to important matters, the king made his wishes known and his mother followed suit. She definitely didn't concern herself with matters pertaining to the rule of Ourlane. Kara would have to see that the future of Ourlane was really of no concern to her.

He walked back into his makeshift quarters and found her standing beside the bench where he'd punished her. Her back was to him and he saw in the daylight the angry marks he'd left on her backside. Her light-brown skin didn't show bruises as much as someone with fairer skin might, but he could still see small traces.

Between the angry red bruises on her behind and the black and blue bruises on her beautiful face, he felt a strange tug in his heart.

He hadn't known who she was when he struck her. But the way she was able to inspire such overwhelming emotion in him should have been a clue. The thought he'd actually made fun of Rohan for not immediately recognizing his mate just a few nights ago ran through his head.

He never would have thought she would come waltzing her tall, lean, taut brown body into his camp with her seductive scent and irritating beliefs.

You should have recognized your mate and you shouldn't have struck her or any woman like that, he chided himself. He knew he would never be able to forgive himself for striking her. The spanking she deserved; and she would get more of them if she dared to disobey him. But the bruises on her lovely face would haunt him for some time to come.

"Good morning," he said softly as he walked up behind her.

She turned and glowered at him but did not respond in greeting. "I see you have found my uncle and his men. What do you plan to do with them?"

Back to The Resistance again. Did she think of nothing else? What would he have to do to remove those thoughts from her mind? "They will be taken to the castle and the king will decide their punishment. After their years of constant treason, I don't have to tell you what will likely be their fate. But that should be of no concern to you."

"How dare you. Of course it's of concern to me. He's my uncle. They are my friends. My people. Their cause is my cause. As long as I have breath in my lungs, I will champion the cause of The Resistance. It's a noble cause to want freedom from tyranny and I know that more intimately than anyone now."

Her brown eyes danced with passion and concern for the rebels. Hissing the words, she turned her back to him and he felt a sharp piercing in his heart.

Taking a deep breath, he tried to contain his growing temper. If only she showed half that much concern for his feelings, then she might see how her lack of loyalty to their union troubled him.

"You have been given a lot of flexibility because of *who* you are. But make no mistake, my dear mate, I lived for years believing I would never have a mate, believing you were dead. And while the thought of living out my days without you broke my heart to the core, I realized I could do so. If you continue on this path of treason and disrespect for all that I hold dear, you won't have to worry about living with tyranny." He whispered the words in her ear and felt her despair.

To her credit his veiled threat did not halt her for long. "You hold things dear and so do I, *Your Highness*. I would no more expect you to shy away from what you believe than I would expect or accept from myself. If you hope I will tow the party line and defend the throne, when I have seen what the greed of the monarchy has done to the people, then you might just as well have me hung with my uncle and the rest of The Resistance."

His eyes narrowed. What had he done to make the Divine send him such a mate? Maybe The Resistance knew what they were doing after all and the woman would surely be the death of him. "Not before you do your duty and provide the heirs I need."

She turned and faced him then, her eyes searched his and she finally took a deep shuddering breath. "I'd like to see my uncle. He needs to know that I didn't betray him on—"

Her words snapped something inside of him and he could not allow her to finish.

"So you rush to assure him of your loyalty even as that act betrays me, your true mate?" Anger pushed forth from him with such shocking force he could barely contain it. His hands gripped her shoulders and he could see each spot where his fingers bit into tender flesh. He loosened his hold a bit and took a deep calming breath, which failed to work.

Her eyes widened and she tried to pull away. He shook her and continued to shake her until he felt a sharp acute pain in his chest. He stopped. A piercing pain unlike anything he'd ever felt shot through his heart. Surely he was going mad dealing with this woman. She would try the patience of a saint or even the most Divinely inspired prophets. How could he, a Warrior Prince, used to having everyone do exactly what he wished, possibly deal with such an infuriating woman?

"You must learn to obey. You must stop testing me in this way, Kara. I don't like hurting you. The longer we are together, the more bonded we will become. When I hurt you, I will feel it worse than you, and when you hurt me, you will feel it worse than me. Tell me you do not feel my heart breaking right now."

She gazed up at him with her tear-filled eyes, and he knew within seconds that she was crying because she felt his hurt at her betrayal and the feeling overwhelmed her.

Even though she felt it, she still wanted to see her uncle. He felt her confusion.

"Can't I just . . ."

"No, Kara!" The woman pushed him beyond his limits. He walked over, grabbed her clothing and handed them to her. "Put these on. I need you to get ready to leave. We have to head out for the castle shortly."

Stamping her foot, she narrowed her eyes. "I wo—"

Darwu clenched his teeth before cutting her off. He could only take so much and she seemed determined to push until he reached the brink of his sanity. "Kara, you will get dressed now and you will leave this compound with me. We are going to the castle where my father, the King of Ourlane, will pass his judgment on your uncle and his followers. As my sacred mate and the future Queen of Ourlane, you will stand with my family and me during this great time when the traitors to Ourlane and the Crown have finally been brought to justice. Is that clear?"

Snatching the clothing from his hand, she took a step back. She hurriedly put the clothing on and started towards the door. He followed her out and watched as she passed his men and kept walking towards the cells on wheels that held her uncle and the other traitors.

Kara.

She kept walking and didn't turn around in response.

Kara!

Still paying him no mind, she pressed forward.

Kara, do not speak to the prisoners.

He spoke the warnings in her mind so as not to call attention to her disobedience in front of the prisoners and his men. But he wanted to yell out her name and stamp his feet in frustration.

She continued to ignore him.

Kara, this is your last warning. Do not make me punish you in front of these men.

She turned, glared at him, and glanced back toward the cells holding her uncle and the others. *I need to see my uncle.*

Her thoughts irritated him to no end and it was all he could do not to snatch her back.

Darwu could care less about her foolish needs, especially as her needs would shame him in front of his men and bring dishonor to the throne. *If you take another step, my mate, you will leave me no other choice but to punish you accordingly.*

Her eyes narrowed. She turned and continued her progression towards the cells.

He took three giant steps and caught her by her hair just as she made it to the front of the cells. Her uncle Rafe glanced at Darwu's hand but Kara didn't even turn. She kept her eyes on her uncle.

"Uncle, I'm very sorry that . . . Ahhhh . . ."

Darwu yanked her hair in a threatening manner. "Do not say another word, Kara." Speaking the words softly in her ears so as not to draw anymore attention to the scene, Darwu hoped the woman would take heed.

"Uncle, I . . . Ohhhhhhh . . ." A hiss escaped her lips as Darwu used his grip on her hair to pull her away from the cell. She refused to heed, so she had to be taught to understand.

Darwu noticed Rafe's eyes never left him and he didn't bother looking at his niece at all even as she tried her best to talk to him.

Remembering vividly the way the older man had struck him when he was fifteen, he took pleasure in seeing the man behind bars. If Rafe hadn't interfered, Darwu would have taken Kara back to the castle. And then she wouldn't have spent the last ten years with those rebels. In fact, Darwu mused, by all rights he should kill Rafe himself for filling Kara's head with all that rebel resistance nonsense.

This is your own fault, Kara. I warned you. You refused to listen and now you will be punished. Darwu dragged his mate back into his quarters and over to the bench. Yanking down her pants he quickly commenced the spanking she so richly deserved.

He knew he could have and very well should have punished her in front of everyone since it was her choice to disrespect him and the throne in front of everyone. But he could not find it in himself to punish her in such a public manner.

Each time his palm struck her bottom he felt his heart breaking. Initially she didn't move or make a sound. But as the punishment wore on she began to cry out and beg him to stop. He couldn't. She had to learn.

When her cries became whimpers and her struggling body went limp on his lap, he stopped. He pulled up her pants, cradled her in his arms and carried her out to the waiting carriage. As he stepped in side, he realized she would never be able to make the long ride to the castle on her sore bottom. So he laid her belly down across his lap for the ride. Resting his head on the back of the seat he closed his eyes.

Kara couldn't stop the tears. She could count on one hand the other times in her life she ever cried. She had found her sacred mate, a time that was supposed to be the happiest time in her life, and she had already doubled the number of times she'd ever cried. That didn't make any sense at all.

She couldn't help feeling like a failure. The Resistance was compromised severely and her uncle would surely be killed. She couldn't have him go to his death thinking she had willingly aligned with the enemy. That she had turned against him and all that he had taught her. She had to find a way to let him know.

Why? Why did her uncle send her to Darwu knowing who he was? Did her uncle know the power Darwu wielded over her? What reason would he have in using her sacred connection to Darwu to kill him. She felt in her soul her uncle would never dishonor a sacred union in such a way.

"Kara, you have to stop." Darwu's eerily calm voice sounded strange to her ears, especially since she was so in tune with his emotions and knew he was anything but calm.

She couldn't sit, doubted she would be able to sit without pain for days. She wanted to hate him. Slowly she got up from his lap and sat as far away from him as she could in the wagon. Pain pulsed through her as soon as her behind touched the seat. Physical pain she could stand. Letting her eyes gaze through the window, she watched as they left the bush and headed into Ourlane. The broken buildings, hinted at a civilization very different from the one they lived in, looked like slivers of silver against the purple backdrop of the sky. Particles of a past she would never fully know or understand haunted her because she knew whatever evil, anger and greed that had infiltrated and destroyed the past world, could do the same to theirs.

The closer they came to the inner Providence the more she allowed her eyes to take in. Other times she'd gone into Ourlane from the bush, she'd done so covertly. She hadn't had time to really look at her people and admire their beauty. Now as they passed through the villages, the people stopped whatever they were doing to bow and otherwise pay tribute to the wagon they knew carried some member of the royal family and salute an army that participated in their oppression. Kara couldn't help but wonder if she would be able to help them more in her new role.

Taking in the beautiful faces that ran from shades of the deepest mahogany to the tawniest of taupe, the people of Ourlane made up a pallet of browns. The women wore their hair of varying textures and hues in braids and twists. The men, most sturdy and strong, all wore the standard cotton work clothes of the commoners. The only thing distinguishing one from the other was their ages and their expressions. The younger men still exhibited a sense of hope the older men had given up long ago.

Staring at the row of children bowing by the side of the road, she noticed that the majority of them wore pieced together rags. Some of them seemed to be malnourished. The homes in the background of the sad picture were barely standing. Some people begrudgingly stopped working in order to pay tribute. There seem to be no joy or happiness, not even when the children waiting for the wagon to pass started playing again. She noticed some of the men in the outer providence shook their heads with sadness as they watched the wagon filled with The Resistance leaders. If the people were really pleased with their lot, wouldn't they have been cheering at the capture of her uncle and the others?

The further they got into the Providence the better things appeared for the people. While none of them lived in luxury, the land was better. And the people had a little more in material wealth. The homes seemed a little sturdier and the children a little better fed. They seemed to have more, but the way the unfair tax system of Ourlane worked, that only meant they probably paid more. Their clothing seemed a little finer. The women wore wraps of fine Kente cloth and the men's work suits were a little better made. They also weren't as dirty. Perhaps that was because the closer they were to the castle, the less the people had to work to till the land. Not all of them had to, apparently. Some of them belonged to the army and otherwise served the throne. They were paid for their loyalty with a somewhat better life. Kara noted that even among these folk there didn't seem to be an abundance of reverence for the throne or joy at the capture of The Resistance.

No, the cause of The Resistance was a noble one. As she watched the people of Ourlane, she knew more than ever her cause was just. She couldn't believe her mate was so blind. He had punished her just for trying to speak to her uncle and didn't know if she would ever be able to forgive him for that.

If her thoughts about the people of Ourlane bothered Darwu, he hadn't shown it, but the mere move to her uncle seemed to make his blood boil.

"I did warn you not to disobey me. I told you not to approach the prisoners or to try and champion their cause. You did so anyhow and now you have the nerve to be riding to meet the king and queen of the Ourlane for the first time worrying about how you will be able to make amends with those traitors in The Resistance."

She thought she heard his voice crack and felt her heart break at the same moment. Surely the Divine would not link her heart, her very soul to the man she was raised to hate. Why would such a fate befall her? She was sure she would never understand. She only knew that if she could somehow soothe the prince's heart and his troubled spirit without turning her back on her uncle, The Resistance and all she held dear, she surely would.

Chapter 5

Kara had never seen anything as ostentatious as the castle. The large grey stones and enormous marble pillars making up the outer façade of the building made for a menacing first look. As she considered all the abject poverty she'd seen in the outer Providence, and the small, homes held together by stray wood, straw, and mud, anger rose in her. Walking up the stairs with the prince, she felt a piece of herself bury itself deeper and deeper with each step—something she knew, intuitively, to hide. Something so deep inside pressed and pressed until she felt small, almost a fraction of herself.

While she had no idea what she would encounter once she entered the huge steel doors of the castle, she could not shake the feeling that she needed to protect herself and her beliefs. If her mate couldn't see why she felt so passionately about things that needed profound change, then the rest of the royals wouldn't be able to understand either.

The huge doors burst open as soon as Kara and the prince reached the second stair from the top. One of the most beautiful women Kara had ever seen stepped out along with a huge hulk of a man. She had a tall and regal appearance. Her dark skin was flawless and her figure strong and shapely. He stood taller than her and had the same muscular and masculine build as Darwu. Both wore elegant apparel and were draped in the finest fabrics. The bejeweled headpieces they wore signaled to her that she was getting her first look at the King and Queen of Ourlane. When the woman ran down the steps and grabbed Darwu in a tight embrace, Kara knew she was right.

"My son! My son! My prayers have been answered. I hope you're done fighting and home for good. Let the army handle the rebels so that you can remain safe." The queen spread kisses all over Darwu and held on to him as if letting go would make him disappear. She clutched him as if her life depended on it.

Kara couldn't help but be impressed with how beautiful the queen appeared. The high cheekbones, almond eyes, and full lips had a presence in real life only hinted at in any artistic rendering Kara had ever seen. The long, silk and lace gown she wore clung to her figure in a seductive manner. Standing next to the powerful king, the queen almost seemed like the absolute perfect companion, the perfect mate for a man so powerful.

"Mother," Prince Darwu whispered as he fell easily into the queen's embrace. He turned his head slightly and acknowledged the king, "Father."

"Son." The king spoke the word to Darwu, but Kara noticed the man never took his eyes off her. His gaze was at the same time penetrating and threatening and sent a shiver down her spine. For a minute his eyes seemed to take on a bright yellow glow.

Kara blinked rapidly when she noticed his eyes were actually a rich dark brown like Darwu's. The sound of her heartbeat raced and gave off a loud thud she was sure everyone around them could hear. She mused that although she considered herself a warrior who had never known fear, her reaction to the King of Ourlane was probably about as close to it as she would get.

Darwu followed the king's gaze and the queen did as well. When the queen's eyes fell on Kara, and her hand went immediately to her mouth. She stepped away from Darwu and walked slowly over to Kara.

"Oh my goodness. You look just like my childhood friend Sara Millan. It's uncanny how much you resemble—" The queen started before Darwu interrupted her.

"Mother, this is Kara Millan, Sara was her mother—"

"Oh my. Oh my! You're alive!" The queen grabbed Kara in a snug embrace and kissed both sides of her cheek. She turned to the king. A strange smile came across the queen's face as she stared at the king. Kara couldn't place the weird expression. "Our son has his true mate, his sacred heart, his destined one. What a joyous day indeed. Not only has our son has returned, but he has brought his future mate with him. This is a cause for celebration. Where were you child? We thought you'd died with the rest of the village."

Besides hardly remembering the day her family and village died, she knew she probably shouldn't tell the king and queen of Ourlane that she'd spent the past ten years getting ready for the revolution to overthrow the monarchy. They wouldn't appreciate the irony of the situation. Since she had no idea how to answer the woman, she just looked at her before turning a questioning glance to Darwu.

The queen raised her hand to Kara's cheek and frowned. "What happened to your beautiful face? Why is it so badly bruised?" The queen glanced from Kara to Darwu. "Did you save the princess from some horrible fate? Tell me you have severely punished the man who would dare harm such a beautiful face?"

Kara noted the look of shame that briefly crossed Darwu face and she shrugged. If those stupid soldiers had not been holding her and she hadn't been so caught off guard by her reaction to the Warrior Prince, he would have never touched her. She was a warrior, too, and figured she would have gotten in some punches of her own. Certain that she could fight with as much battle skill as her mate, she tried to concentrate on not blurting out how lucky the prince had been she hadn't been free to hit him back.

The king's eyes narrowed. "How do we know she really is who she claims to be?"

"I know my mate, Father." Darwu bit out his words and his back straightened as his chest bulked up considerably.

The king observed Kara carefully and his eyebrow slanted. "Did you know her when you struck her and caused those bruises?"

Kara blinked and took a step backward. His eyes glowed yellow again. The pressing in her chest came back double-fold and she had the urge to hide. She felt as though she'd seen the glowing yellow eyes before—but where? They looked almost evil and…just like that they were gone. Shaking her head briefly, she focused on Darwu.

Shame and indignation crossed the prince's face with rapid speed. "Clearly, I didn't!"

Waving his hand, in a dismissive manner, the king responded, "Then how can you know? And where has she been hiding all these years?"

Darwu glanced around. Kara watched him, figuring he must have noticed most of the servants outside had stopped what they were doing and were paying close attention to their conversation. "We need to move this discussion indoors. There is much to discuss and the front steps of the castle is not the best place."

The queen glanced from her son to her husband and nodded. She kept one arm around Kara and used the other to pat Darwu on the back. "Yes, let's go inside to talk and become acquainted with our newfound daughter."

Kara followed them inside, all the while keeping her eyes on the king. Something at the pit of her warrior's gut whispered to her to be careful and not turn her back on him. She had to figure out where she had seen the glowing yellow eyes before. That is if he really had glowing yellow eyes and she really saw what she thought she saw. She couldn't explain the feeling he gave, but knew she'd never felt so uneasy in all her life.

What sort of foolishness are you thinking up now, woman?

Kara ignored the prince and his flippant questions. She hadn't been thinking her thoughts to him or about him and she resented his occupation of her mind.

"We can talk in my personal chambers," the king snapped as they followed him inside.

Kara let her eyes roam the outlandishly lavish interior of the castle. Drapes of silk lined the windows. Even the hallways had rich wool rugs and fine artistic renderings of the royal family hung on the walls. Everything in the castle screamed 'the finest.' The finest woods, the finest fabrics, the finest materials. *So this is what the blood of the people is supporting,* she thought as an angry hiss escaped her lips.

The queen turned at the sound. "Is something wrong, dear?"

Taking a deep breath, Kara forced a smile. "Nothing, Your Majesty. I'm just taking in your home. I've never been inside anything like it. Most of the people of Ourlane probably have never seen a tenth of what is so abundant here."

Kara . . . a low warning grumble echoed in her head. *Do not start.* Although Darwu's tone was soft his demeanor was anything but soothing.

"You probably find this to be a bit much," the king said with a smirk as they entered the door to his chambers. "My guess is that you are one of those bleeding heart sympathizers who pleads the cause of the people every chance she gets. Am I right?"

Glancing around at the sturdy wood, and rich tapestries, Kara knew the only one way she could answer the king was truthfully. The exploitive display of wealth offended all of her sensibilities.

"Guilty as charged, I'm afraid, Your Highness." She barely got the words out before she felt a sharp pain shoot from one temple to the other. The piercing pain lasted for a matter of seconds before it stopped. She glanced up and noticed Darwu glaring at her. Had he caused the pain?

There will be more pain than that small throbbing if you do not hold your tongue, woman! Darwu's eyes narrowed ever so slightly.

Do not threaten me! I will not be bullied into maintaining a façade of pleasantness when everything about this overly decadent castle disgusts me! Kara massaged her temple and glared at Darwu.

67

If you persist, my dear sweet mate, you will leave me no choice but to bring you to heel. Darwu's expression promised he would be all too happy to carry out his threat.

The indignation she felt at his words pulsed through her body and she had to stop herself from leaping on him and pummeling his hard muscled frame. *I am not an animal that you can train. I am a woman, a warrior. And I promise you this, mate of mine, I will not bend to your will easily, if at all. I have a mind of my own. And if you are going to keep me here and away from the cause of my people, then you better get used to it.*

Kara watched as the arrogant prince glared at her and noted the king and queen watched them with interest.

"Are you two communicating with one another telepathically? How romantic. I remember when the king and I first mated. His ability to connect with me and live in my head was so new to him. He couldn't get enough of whispering sweet and darn right scandalous thoughts in my mind. It was truly a wonderful time. And then I gave birth to Darwu and gained the ability to truly know the king's mind. It was even more amazing." The queen spoke in a breathless gush and stared longingly at the king.

Kara tried hard not to puke. If the queen thought for one second Kara liked having Darwu privy to her every thought, she really needed to think again. And the idea of becoming pregnant and adding another member to the royals was far removed from anything she would even consider.

"Listen, Father, Mother, let us get on with this so that Kara and I can get some rest after our long journey from the bush. We need to get a head start making the heirs to continue our family legacy and rule of Ourlane." Darwu narrowed his gaze daring her to speak.

Kara closed her eyes and swallowed her words. The energy of the castle along with the disturbing vibes she got from the king overwhelmed her. The last thing she needed to do was anger her mate. As irritating as he was, he seemed to be the only thing standing between her and death.

And death seemed to be all around her, clawing at her from the walls, as if all the decadence and design was meant to cover up something. She had no idea what. She only knew that castle made her uncomfortable, even the warrior in her felt a little afraid as they walked down the dark halls. They entered a large chamber decorated with rich tapestries and silks. Huge paintings of each of the former Kings of Ourlane hung on the walls. The evil seemed to grow stronger and stronger from one picture to the next. As Kara took in the piercing gaze of the current king, something told her that she might be looking at the most evil of them all. Fear, which she had been blissfully free of most of her life in the bush, returned.

Sit down, Kara. No one is going to hurt you here. Just watch yourself. Do not do or say anything to offend the king and queen. Darwu pulled a chair out for her and she sat down.

The king and queen sat down directly in front of them. The throbbing of her bottom as it touched the wood of the chair reminded her of the cost of defying Darwu. She didn't think she would be able to pay such a price so soon after the last, so she tried her best to hold her tongue.

"So son, do tell me what makes you so overly certain this young woman is your sacred mate. How can we be sure she is not part of some elaborate Resistance hoax? I mean really, the entire village was destroyed." The king gave her a piercing glare.

Kara wrapped her arms around herself and looked the king dead in the eye. His eyes glowed yellow again and she looked away. As she did she caught the hint of the bright red sun beaming through the large windows of the castle. Some people had eye colors that changed in the sunshine, she mused. The other time she thought she'd seen it they were outside. That had to be it. Willing her heart to stop pounding so loudly and trying to push back her fear, she turned her gaze back to the king. She glimpsed a hazy red fog encasing him. As soon as she focused in on it, it disappeared. As she tried to tell herself she'd imagined it, a chill settling in her bones told her otherwise.

Darwu let out a sigh before responding. "Father, I know the village was destroyed. I was there."

The king bolted up sharply in his seat. "What do you mean you were there?"

"I heard you telling mother The Resistance planned to ambush the village containing my future sacred mate. You said there would be no way the army could make it to the village in time. I went there—"

"But you were only a child yourself. What did you hope to do but get yourself killed?" The queen patted her chest and her face took on a pained and troubled expression.

Eyes narrowed, the king still seemed skeptical. "Why are you telling us this now?"

"Because I found her, and I tried to get her to leave with me. Her uncle and the rest of The Resistance came and knocked me unconscious. When I came to, they were gone and so was she. I thought they had killed her, that I had failed." Darwu took a sharp breath before continuing. "I realize now The Resistance was already planning back then to use her against me in some way."

"That is not true. I told you they simply wanted to talk to you about a truce." Kara couldn't contain herself any longer. If they were going to hear the story, she wanted them to be privy to the entire story. The Resistance kept her alive, taught her to fight, and gave her a reason to live after losing everyone close to her. They were her family.

Shut up, Kara. Darwu warned her telepathically.

The king shot her look that seemed to echo the words Darwu spoke in her mind. He turned to his son. "So, son, if you were knocked out, how do you know she wasn't killed? You have no proof The Resistance did not finish the job they had started." The king paused and sneered at Kara before continuing. "And why on earth didn't you tell me years ago. If any chance existed that the girl survived then we needed to know."

"Why did you need to know?" Kara bit the words out harshly.

Taken aback, the king turned to Kara, but didn't respond. His eyes didn't glow yellow, but he did appear angry and annoyed.

She told herself the sunshine had made his eyes that evil putrid shade.

"Well, so that we could rescue you of course, dear." The queen was the first of the royal couple to come up with an answer to Kara's query. "I for one don't need any proof of who you are. I knew your mother." She smiled a smile that never quite reached her slightly slanted eyes. "You look exactly like her. I swear you even have her aura. It's uncanny, really."

"You should have told us about this son." The king snapped.

"I know. But as I said, I didn't want to share my failure. And then the dreams . . ." Dawru started and then faltered off.

"What dreams, son?" Intrigued, the queen leaned forward.

"They were nothing really. I've just had these reoccurring dreams about that day pretty much since the time it happened. But they were always from her eyes, the way she must have seen and felt it." Darwu responded hesitantly before glancing at everyone in the room. Kara could only assume he felt weird about sharing his dreams with everyone or maybe felt strange about having them at all.

"Oh, I wish you had told us about these dreams, son!" The queen beamed as she clasped her hands together. "If you were dreaming of her through her eyes, the Divine was letting you know she was still alive."

"Well, apparently she is who she claims to be." The king offered grudgingly. "But that does not mean she can be trusted. She has had years with The Resistance. She could very well slit our throats while we sleep. I know she is your mate son, but I'm afraid—"

"I have been in her head father. I know her mind. I know her heart. She does have misguided views about the monarchy, but she is not going to kill us." Darwu's tone and stance brokered no argument. The firm timbre of his voice impressed Kara more than she wanted to be at that moment.

Especially since she thought him presumptuous to say with such certainty she wished the monarchy no harm. She most certainly wanted the monarchy to end.

The king didn't give in easily. "You can be so sure even with your mother's life at stake?"

And neither did Darwu. "I am certain, Father."

The king stared at Kara. She noted the venom pulsing through his gaze and knew that if he could find a way to make it happen, he could certainly kill her.

Don't be foolish, Kara. My father does not want you dead. He knows what you mean to the continued reign of his bloodline, Darwu snapped in her head.

The reality of just what she meant to them hit her with a force she couldn't name, much less stand. She rejected the concept as soon as it registered. She would never bring a child into this evil castle. She would never allow her body to be used as a vessel to insure the continued reign of the corrupt monarchy.

Enough, Kara! Darwu's voice hissed in her head. *Do you think you will have a choice?*

A chill ran through her and her heart stilled. She had a choice. Didn't she? By all that was Divine she had a choice and she would rather choose death than the destiny dangling in front of her. She had beliefs. She had a cause. She would always uphold them. *Always.*

She turned to face her sacred mate who looked as if he were about to explode. His bright brown eyes were rounded and his nostrils flared. She could feel the anger and hurt rolling off him assaulting her senses, unlike anything she'd ever experienced. Her heart started throbbing and she turned away thinking it might somehow lessen the effect. It did not.

"Mother and Father, I hope you have enough answers to your questions for now. As I said before, it has been a long and tiresome journey home. And my time spent in the bush fighting The Resistance has left me longing for the comfort of my quarters, even more so now that I have found my sacred mate. If you will excuse us, we will turn in and begin making the future heirs of Ourlane." Darwu gave Kara a pointed look. "If we do not make it down to dinner, please forgive us in advance and have the cook send something to our quarters." Standing, he held out his hand for Kara.

Glancing at the strong hand and firmly muscled arm reaching out for her, Kara instantly got up from her chair. Her automatic response to Darwu and seemingly ingrained desire to do his will grated her nerves. The slant of his eyes and the tilt of his smile let her know he was just trying to figure out the boundaries of their connection and the limits of his impact on her.

"Fine son, I guess we have to accept this for now and know that somehow, your little mate has survived for a reason." The king said the words and Kara wondered if she was the only one who could tell he didn't mean them. "But do try and make it down for dinner. Your uncle and your cousins will no doubt want to see you. They are collecting the taxes in Ourlane and the outer providences and are expected back this evening."

Darwu simply nodded at his father's request and walked out of the room, bidding Kara to follow with a curt, stilted *come* spoken in her head.

The hair on the back of Kara's neck stood up and her skin prickled. More than the murderous Warrior Prince, The Resistance hated the thieving malicious tax collecting team made up of Prince Alto and his sons Princes Jorge and Gab. While the Warrior Prince was ruthless in battle at least he'd been known to fight fair.

Fair with the exception of siphoning the brain of his sacred mate to find out the location of The Resistance, Kara thought wryly. Perhaps he was cut from the same cloth as the rest of the royals and her uncle had been foolish to think they could negotiate with him. If only her uncle hadn't sent her to the enemy.

Darwu halted his steps and turned to face her. His piercing gaze caused a shudder to trail down her spine. *There is a certain down-side to being privy to your every thought, mate! For surely you think*

Divine Destiny

too much and think all the wrong things. *While it may prove interesting, indeed challenging, to get you to see the error of your ways listening to this constant drivel about your murderous uncle and the pack of outlaws you call The Resistance is wearing dangerously thin.*

She almost let his rant go unchallenged but the warrior in her refused to be silenced. *Well the fact that I apparently have no choice but to live here among people I have been raised to abhor, to watch the continued rape and pillage of the people and the land, when I would rather be fighting oppression until my dying breath is my fate. So why should you get off any easier?*

His eyes narrowed. He outstretched his hand, clearly intending for her to take it. She huffed and hurried past him only slowing once she realized she had no idea where they were headed. As Darwu continued his angry trek down the hall, she followed.

Chapter 6

Darwu had never felt more torn in all his life. His mate was miserable and clearly determined to make him miserable as well. He felt her pain and the inner turmoil being in the castle caused her. If he could have let her go he would. He didn't enjoy seeing her in pain and seeing her so conflicted.

But the only way to end the pain she felt would be the equivalent of ripping out his heart. He was astonished that he felt so strongly for her in such a short amount of time. He loved her. Each minute he felt the love and desire growing stronger and stronger coupled with an overwhelming need to breed. He'd never let her go free.

She was bonded to him. He had to find a way to resign her to her fate. He needed her to know he loved her. He needed her to stop testing him!

The Divine had a reason for sanctioning the monarchy throughout the generations. The Resistance had not only gone against Ourlane, they'd defiled all that was sacred with their treasonous acts against the throne. If the monarchy were wrong, surely the Divine would cause its downfall. His family wouldn't have been able to lead for so many generations. No, the monarchy was right. The Resistance was wrong.

Opening the door to his suite, Darwu turned and glanced at Kara. Her beauty took his breath away. Even though she took every chance she could to irritate him, he found he couldn't stay angry with her for long. He simply wasn't built that way. He was baffled, especially since he had spent the past ten years of his life holding a grudge and waging war against The Resistance.

He watched as she cautiously entered the suite. The gentle sway of her hips beckoned him in ways he'd never experienced before. He would never be able to give her up, not even for her happiness. The sooner she became used to her new fate, the better.

He felt her apprehension as she surveyed the enormous outer room. Like the rest of the castle, his quarters were lavish and opulent. Seeing his home through her eyes caused him a discomfort he was unaccustomed to. They were the royal family after all; it was only right the castle be filled with the richness of the land. He shouldn't have felt any guilt and he reasoned that he didn't. Kara and her foolish ideas about the rebels had infiltrated his brain. Her influence gave him all the more reason to bring her into line as quickly as possible.

"We will bathe, and retire for a brief nap. Then, depending on how we're feeling later we can go down and have dinner with my parents." He spoke in an easy tone hoping to lighten the mood.

Kara's eyes widened. "Bathe . . . together?"

Amazed by how innocent and inexperienced his little Resistance fighter was, he responded, "Yes. There is a large bathing pool in the suite. I'm sure the servants have already prepared it for our use. They know I like to relax into a nice bath when I return from battle. Come." He gestured for her to follow him to the back of the suite.

The bathing pool bubbled with steamy water. The tropical scents of Ourlane wafted through the air. All the flowers of the land filled the room and petals pulsed in the water. The sweet scent, along with the subtle hint of desire coming from Kara intoxicated him. Darwu turned to Kara and began to undress her. The skin on the back of his neck prickled and his breath caught at the sight of her lithe brown body. Every curve, every crevice seemed to call out to him. The smell of willow, rose, seduction and desire beckoned him as his hands explored her.

Lifting his hand to her nipple, he enclosed the pointed tip between his thumb and forefinger and pulled slightly. She let out a hiss of air and he bent his head taking the other nipple firmly in his mouth. He tugged one breast with his fingers as he slowly sank his teeth into the other. *You are beautiful, Kara. I don't think I will ever get enough of you.*

Kara's head fell back. "My. Darwu."

She was so responsive to his touch he thought he might come just from teasing her nipples and watching her orgasm. He suckled more intensely and her knees buckled beneath her. Catching her and lifting her up into his arms, he carried her over to the bathing pool. He placed her inside the soothing water, sitting her on the stone bench. Removing his wet clothing as quickly as he could, he joined her in the bath, taking a seat next to her on the submerged bench.

He sensed immediately the return of her apprehension and knew he had to do something to get her to submit to their fate. Deciding it would be more prudent to show her the benefits of a union between them, he bent his head and took her lush mouth with his.

Placing her hands on his chest, she tried to push him away, but he used them to pull her closer to him. He felt her body relax just as her tongue began to chart its own path in his mouth. Letting his hand play with her nipples, he found each squeeze brought soft moans from her. He moved to her soft, slick center.

Just being near her caused his heart to beat rapidly. Hardly able to contain his excitement, he took a breath and then another. Each breath inhaled and exhaled brought the drug of her scent to him full force. His pulse quickened all the more.

Probing her with two fingers, he used his thumb to tease her clit while his fingers worked her and soon she was grinding her hips ever so pleasingly against his hand. Her eyes began to flutter and her head went back as she tried to suppress her cries. She looked gorgeous when she came.

Taking a deep breath, he bent his head to her ear and whispered. "I need you more than I need air, my mate."

She stared at him blankly for a moment, still in the throes of passion; she appeared torn. Wrapping his arms around her, he pulled her unto his lap so that she straddled him.

"I want you so bad I ache. You want me, too." He had to make her see that things could work. Divine mates weren't made lightly. Their connection was as solid and as real as anything he had ever experienced. He held her hips steady as he lifted his own and thrust inside of her.

The combination of her warm, tight sheath and the bubbling warm water surrounding them sent his senses into overload. "Do you see, Kara? Do you see that we are meant to be together? That nothing should come between us? The sooner you accept this, the sooner you accept your place in the royal family, the better our lives will be." He thrust his hips upwards and a sharp moan escaped her lips.

She gritted her teeth and grounded her pelvis into his. "Why am I the only one who has to accept things? Why can't you accept me for who I am? For what I believe?"

Darwu closed his eyes and absorbed the velvet tightness of her sharp strokes and pulls. She bounced down, impaling herself over and over again.

Kara worked her hips delectably and diligently. "Shouldn't it work both ways, Darwu? Can't it work both ways? We have to find a way to really accept each other or our union won't work."

Darwu grabbed her hips and held her before silencing her with a kiss. He couldn't let her take over his plans for seducing her. If he let her continue to talk while she rotated those glorious hips and squeezed him in her viselike, moist tightness, the Divine only knew what he would agree to.

He swallowed her lips and her words in a probing kiss, feeling he could very well kiss her forever. The more he tasted, the more he wanted to taste. Sinking his teeth in gently he pulled her lower lip with a possessive tug.

As he held her hips still, he thrust up with fervor and she came apart in his arms. A low keening sound passed from her gut out of her mouth and into his. Her explosion ricocheted through her and spread to him. Soon he found sweet release as his seed spurted into her.

He held her afterward and then he bathed her. Once they dried off he carried her to the bed. Placing her gently on the soft bed, he plopped down, relishing the feel of the comfortable mattress after months of sleeping on a pallet.

"You're not even going to try are you?" The hurt he heard in her voice gave him pause. She spoke the words in such a defeated tone he almost wished he could find a way to meet her halfway. But how could he?

"No, Kara. I'm not going to try because I know I'm right. The Divine wouldn't have sanctioned the rule of my family throughout the years, bringing Ourlane through years and years of hard times and turmoil, if it wasn't right." He offered with only a small piece of hesitation.

"Can you honestly say your family's rule is good for the people of Ourlane? Do you even look at the people as you ride through the villages in your fancy carriages? The people are starving!" Kara sat up in the bed and faced him. "They are barely making ends meet. Some die young leaving others to die alone because their sacred mates are gone. The Divine can't possibly want this for our people."

What in all Divine would it take to tame this woman's tongue? "Be careful. You tread very closely to treason."

"Treason? For what? Stating the facts? The people need more." She let out a hiss, crossed her arms, and rolled her eyes.

Darwu grabbed her face more harshly than he'd intended and glared at her. He couldn't help but narrow his eyes in anger and shake her a little. He was mated to a mad woman. She was determined to have herself hung for treason.

"This is the last time I am going to say this, Kara. Things are the way they are. Nothing you can say or do will change anything. You are my mate. You will bear my children. You will hold your tongue and speak no more of this foolishness about the monarchy, The Resistance, or the *people*. You will button your lips and hold your tongue or I will have it removed. Am I clear?" Trying to talk through clenched teeth wasn't easy. The sharpness of his words surprised him, but he had to find a way to get the woman to see reason. He couldn't lose her again. He wouldn't.

She glared at him and took a deep breath as one lone teardrop fell down her cheek.

He tried to search her mind to see what she was thinking but found it eerily blank. Surely she was thinking something, he thought. Or maybe he had finally scared all of the foolish thoughts out of her head and stunned her into thoughtlessness. *Finally. Peace.* He let go of her cheek and just continued to stare at her daring her to speak or think one of her idiotic rebel thoughts. The sudden welcomed silence of her thoughts and her voice washed over him as he appraised her. He only hoped it would last and he'd gotten all of that Resistance nonsense out of her once and for all.

Kara stared at Darwu's angry face. She had no idea how she'd done it, but she'd managed to find a place in her head Darwu couldn't breach.

Something had clicked in her when he grabbed her face, and everything inside her retreated to the nook in her head as a form of self-preservation. One minute, she felt frightened, even scared, and the next she kicked into warrior mode and started plotting.

Darwu's harsh words made her feel as if she would never be able to hold onto her beliefs or herself living in the castle as his mate. In an attempt to prevent that fate, she called on the Divine, retreated and found a safe haven. Her mental retreat proved to be the best strategy she could use. She'd found a space to hide her thoughts. A space he couldn't get to.

Stupid, insufferable man! Greedy, money hording monarch! Down with the monarchy! Free the land! She could let the thoughts ring loudly from her safe space. The way she had from the time he held onto her chin and lashed out his threats. And just like then, he hadn't detected them. He just sat there looking smug and content that he had stopped her from thinking about her duty and the people.

Breathing a sigh of relief, Kara closed her eyes thinking of how she was going to fight her way out of her Divinely inspired predicament. And she was so happy that Darwu the Warrior Prince had no idea what she was thinking.

Chapter 7

*R*afe my mate, you're here in the castle, so close I can feel you. It pains me that I can't see you. I wish I could sneak and—

Sitting in the dungeon cell with the rest of his men awaiting his fate, Rafe felt a wonderful warmth flow over his body as the words broke through the worries on his mind and he sensed the presence of his sacred mate. He could almost see her jet back hair neatly coiled in twists and her dark dreamy eyes full of devotion. Stopping short of conjuring up the image of her svelte and curvaceous body, Rafe wished he could find a way to touch the love of his life.

Even though they'd lived apart longer than they had together and they had never been able to openly live their lives as a couple, they remained connected. He smiled with his entire body as he answered her via their psychic connection.

Don't risk it, Donia. If you were caught, then all of our sacrifices, all of our years apart would be for nothing. We're too close now.

Donia had been The Resistance's source inside the castle. She was the one who warned him the king and his brother were going to destroy the village in hopes of killing the young shamaness. Between Donia on the inside and Cerrill leaking information to the royals on the outside, The Resistance had been able to keep the royals at bay and protect Kara until she had enough strength to fulfill her destiny.

She's here now. I haven't seen her yet. But there's talk all around the castle of the prince's sacred mate. The way Donia's loving thoughts touched his mind made even the dank and dark cell seem like a bright room filled with a glowing fire.

Rafe was amazed he and Donia had been able to maintain their connections, but the Divine had its reasons and knew the roles he and Donia would have to play in keeping Kara safe.

Even though the once-powerful child hadn't exhibited any of the remarkable powers she had when she was younger, the young shamaness exuded a wealth of power. He could only imagine she had somehow cloaked herself as a form of protection after seeing the village destroyed and her parents killed. She had hidden herself so well he didn't think she knew herself any longer. But he had seen glimpses of her power through the years. Making her a warrior and a freedom fighter helped to contain some of it. But he knew a power so strong couldn't be contained for long.

She'll need you, Donia. That's why you can't risk trying to see me. I have done my part keeping her safe all these years and now she'll need you. She will need allies in this castle. I don't know how you stayed here all these years. I can feel the evil seeping from the walls. Rafe shuddered, shaking off the clawing feeling of what he now knew for certain was the influence of the Cultide.

He'd always sensed that the corruption flowing from the castle across the land had something to do with evil influences. But he'd thought it was more the Cultide using its usual trickery, but the evil in the castle was more than a little fun and games. These people must worship evil in the face of the Divine in order to exude the aura he felt.

His niece faced a bigger battle than he originally anticipated, but he had faith she would triumph. He felt a sigh overcome Donia even though he couldn't see it or hear it.

I know, but hopefully all will end soon. As soon as the shamaness comes into her full power—

Hopefulness captured Donia's spirit that somehow Kara would be able to save him. Rafe had to squelch his mate's desires. *She will still have a lot to work against. I won't be here to help so—*

This time her grief shook him and pierced his heart.

Divine Destiny

Oh, don't say it, Rafe. Isn't there some way? Can't we find a way to— The soft timbre of her plea, so unlike his spunky opinionated mate, saddened him.

Wishing he could grant her wish for a future with the two of them together, he gave her only what their destiny demanded. *No, love. I've done what I was chosen to do. I've done all I can. The rest is up to Kara and her prince.*

Do you think he will come to see the truth and the light? All that she represents? If he doesn't then this truly will all be for nothing. A hint of bitterness seeped into Donia's voice and Rafe couldn't allow it to remain. They had sacrificed much because the prophecies told of what would happen when the one shamaness powerful enough and caring enough to take on the tide of the ruling class and free the people would be born.

Kara fit the prophecy in every way. Even the way she came into her powers, so young and so strong, said she was special. Most shamanesses didn't get their full powers until they were of child-bearing age and even then they were usually glimmers and flickers.

A Shamaness, not destined to be a royal mate, had years to grow into power and become vital to their village. Most villages depended on a shamaness for healing and guidance. A royal shamaness usually ended up with her power corrupted and destroyed, or if those in power thought she couldn't be corrupted, she was killed.

Kara was so strong as a ten-year-old child she had saved herself from death. Rafe had to believe she would come into herself in enough time to bring freedom once and for all, so that all of their sacrifices would be worth it.

No. It wouldn't. She is still who she is and who she was destined to be. With him, her power is greater and true. And with him she will blossom rapidly. But she is still the chosen and she is still meant to lead and bring the new day. The prince is her sacred mate. He may fight it, but in time he won't be able to help but see her for who she truly is.

Ideally, the king and his chosen shamaness ruled together. Though it had never been so in his lifetime, Rafe read forbidden versions of the Divine prophecies and he knew what the Divine intended. The king was not meant to rule the land with corrupt advisors but with a strong and sacred mate. Corrupting the power of a shamaness and killing those who couldn't be changed went against all that was Divine. It reeked of the Cultide.

Donia broke through his thoughts once again and the sound of her voice soothed him. *I hope you're right and I wish that happens in time to spare your life, my love. I don't think I can live without you.*

You can and you will. Just think of the cause. And think of the day when you will see our son again. He is safe in the far outer Providences of Ourlane. And one day he is going to need to know who he is and who his parents are. He'll need to know why we sacrificed the chance to raise him. And I'm counting on you to tell him, my love. Rafe sighed. Donia had to live otherwise he could not go to his death in peace.

"Rafe, you've been sitting there silent for hours. I know we are all ready and willing to die for the cause, but seeing Kara suffer so isn't right."

Rafe's head snapped up and he looked at Nic lounging on a makeshift pallet on the floor against the grimy wall. Nic was one of the five other men involved with The Resistance who had been captured by Darwu's army. The tall lanky young man had an angry glare in his face. His handsome brown features were twisted up in a snarl. Rafe knew his niece had experimented a little with the young soldier and therefore Nic's concern ran a little deeper than the man was willing to admit.

Figuring the men needed some form of morale boosting as they sat awaiting their death, Rafe ended his conversation with Donia. *I'll talk with you later this evening, my love. I need to speak with my men now.*

Yes, Rafe. Know that I am with you. Donia always understood and for some reason that made him sad. Had he asked too much of his mate all these years? Bonding with her when they were so young. Sending their child away and allowing her to go off to this evil castle as a spy? Was The Resistance and the change they hoped for worth it?

Yes, my love. Even though I sometimes wish our lives could have been different, if one child can grow up, if our own grandchildren who we may never know, can grow up in a world of peace and freedom, then all is worth it. I love you, Rafe. And just like that Donia was gone.

"What do you mean, Nic? My niece is fine. We're the ones who will be hung in a matter of days." Rafe tried a light-hearted attempt at humor, which brokered no laughter from his comrades and fellow cellmates. All had watched Kara grow up and felt just as protective of her as he did, maybe more so because Rafe had always known deep in his gut and believed with more fervor than anyone that Kara was the one.

Nic let out a huff of air and sat upright in his makeshift seat. "Yes but did you see her face? The way he manhandled her, dragging her off the way he did, when all she wanted to do was speak, to reassure you . . . it's not right!"

"If she really is the special one, the chosen shamaness, she should be treated with reverence, not struck like that!" Bo said between clenched teeth. The muscular cinnamon-colored man's hazel eyes flashed with a wealth of unvoiced threats. "And even if she isn't, she is Kara, our Kara, and had I not been in that cage, I would have killed the—"

"She is the chosen shamaness. And she is a warrior. You men have stood side by side in battle with her." Rafe shook his head incredulously. He couldn't believe his men were so worried about Kara. She could handle herself. They had all trained her. "You've seen her with worse bruises than those the prince gave her. In fact the last time the two of you sparred, Nic, you blacked her eye and it stayed swollen for over a week."

Nic hung his head in shame and Rafe almost felt bad for bringing it up. Nic had felt horrible for weeks after blacking Kara's eye. Even her jokes hadn't made him feel better.

"Oh sure throw that in my face. I hadn't meant to hit her so hard. I didn't even want her as my sparring partner. And she kept provoking me," Nic responded grudgingly.

"Because she wanted to be prepared for whatever battle brings." Rafe offered passionate words he hoped would inspire his men and make them give up the pity hole they were trying to dig. "She is not a wimp. She can handle herself. And because she is the chosen shamaness, she can handle herself better than any of us can. We have done our part, men. The rest is up to her."

"But what if she doesn't evolve? What if she doesn't come into herself?" Scot, who had been sitting quietly off in a corner, suddenly voiced what they all in some form or another had wanted to say. Smaller than any of the other comrades, Scot was also older. The salt-and-pepper gray of his tightly coiled hair bespoke years of wisdom.

Hoping Scot's knowledge was off on this point, Rafe let out a spirit heavy sigh before responding. "Then all of this will have been for nothing."

Chapter 8

Divine Prophecy
Book of Dana (circa 2051)
The lost chapters

Once the Divine's favored ones reconnected and ensured their souls a place in the great beyond, they lived out the rest their days on earth together. They had only one task to make sure that their destinies were fulfilled. That task was to make sure the Divine's chosen people would survive the great war to come, a war that would leave the earth ravished and destitute, changing even the atmosphere and the universe. Man-made weapons destroyed man-made objects. Anything created by the Divine could only be destroyed by the Divine. Her original haven of happiness remains awaiting her chosen. It is Our Land, the land made for us in Divine love.

Her original favored couple finally found one another in the twenty-first century; too late to stop the wars and disease that would ravish the land due to the Cultide's wicked rule. But in enough time to gather followers and find the peace of land on the continent of Africa they believed to be the Promised Land, the place of the Divine's earliest settlers. They lived out their lives there and took their growing village underground when the Great War came.

They passed as much as they could along to the chosen but not everyone is willing to believe the truth. Some truly believed that the Divine was responsible for granting Divine mates. Others believed the chemicals and poisons from the bombs changed the make-up of the people so that they became more adept at recognizing their mates. Some became the unit of co-equal mates the Divine wanted for all. Others allowed the Cultide to seep in and corrupt their unions.

The Cultide continued to try and destroy happiness and create heartache for his sister. She no longer became heartbroken when the Cultide was able to stir up trouble. In their human form, her chosen ones had free will. They could just as easily turn their backs on Divine love, as they could embrace it.

Even within the ranks of those chosen for the new beginning in Our Land, they were not all on the same accord. And wherever the Cultide saw an opening to wreak havoc, he took it and corrupted it to his will.

From the beginning of time, when the Divine gave pieces of her power to all her favored, she had created strong women. Sometimes they called these women healers. Sometimes they were medicine women, root workers, obeah women, and voodoo priestesses. Some worked with herbs and spells. Some could call on the various names that the Divine has been called through the years and will things into being with the power of the word. The Divine found much favor in these women no matter what they were called because they had each found the Divine in themselves, loved it, nurtured it, and spread it to as many as they could.

Throughout time, the women with these Divine attributes always found ways to be useful and to help the cause of justice. A time will come when even those who were given small measures of Divine power will find themselves fighting against an evil so great it will overtake the entire land.

At times, the chosen may feel as if they have been forsaken. Long suffering might cause them to believe the Divine no longer cared. These feelings will be false but the Cultide will cause them to linger. The Divine will send one with the power to save. One who comes from a long line of healers, root workers, and obeah women. One who has only to speak in the name of the Divine and Divine will be done. With power so great it will manifest even when she is a child. She will be the one meant to save.

The Cultide will try and kill this chosen one because she is destined to bring change to all of the chosen in Our Land. The Divine's chosen one will make manifest the true meaning of Our Land. No one group or person has dominion over the land. Destined to free the people and the land. Destined to spread love, happiness, and light. Nothing will corrupt her. Try as he might, the Cultide won't be able to infiltrate her with his evil.

The Cultide will try to kill this very powerful woman. And if she is killed before she can reach adulthood, then the fate of Our Land will be ruined. If she lives and connects with her Divine sacred mate, the one powerful enough to take her on her own terms, *they* will be invincible.

The king placed the prophecy his ancestors had long since taken out of the Divine Chronicles back in the drawer. All the forbidden prophecies were in a hidden place in his secret ritual room. Some of the forbidden prophecies were still out there. Through the years his ancestors had destroyed as many as they could. They only kept one copy for themselves so that they would know what to look for and be able to use it to insure their reign and the continued power of the Cultide. He'd used the prophecy ten years ago to call on the Cultide and locate the village where the enormous power was coming from and he thought his men had been able to destroy it.

After telling his brother the supposed dead girl was indeed alive, he waited to see what Alto had to say for himself. He should have never trusted Alto to lead the men in the destruction of the village. He should have gone himself. Once the spell he cast trying to get a dog to attack and kill the source of the power hadn't worked, he should have gone to the village and snapped the child's neck himself.

"What do you mean she's still alive? That's impossible!" Prince Alto's head snapped up from his relaxed state.

Rolling his eyes in disgust, the king could only glare at his incompetent younger brother. Knowing Alto and his stupid brood would take over the throne after Darwu's rule gave him considerable pause. Maybe little wench's survival was a good thing. If Darwu had an heir, then Alto and his lineage wouldn't be needed after all.

"My son came back with his mate today, brother. A mate who is destined to bring great change to Ourlane. A mate who you assured me was dead!" Sitting back in his chair, King Milo just glared at his brother.

"But you have been a part of every ceremony. You know the Cultide didn't sense her power any longer. We have not felt the threat since the attack on the village. Even now, if she were truly the one, we would have felt something. No way would someone prophesied to have so much power, be able to walk into this castle—a castle protected by the Cultide—and not be sensed. We would have felt something. We would know."

Prince Alto had gotten his lazy, fat behind up from his seat and paced the floor slowly.

The fool was too pathetic to even pace the floor with any semblance of fortitude. "Then how do you account for the fact that she is indeed his mate? And her name is Kara Millan, the daughter of Sara Millan."

"Well, surely, she must be a part of some elaborate trick by The Resistance. Perhaps she is even a witch of some sort. However, if she were practicing any sort of witchcraft we would be able to pick up on that as well . . . I don't know." Puzzled, Prince Alto sat back in his chair. "I really don't know. But I will not rest until we know for sure. She will not ruin everything our great forefathers set in place for our family. Have you thought about having her meet her demise?"

"I have, unless another way is found. But it would have to be an accident and Darwu can never find out." The king rubbed his hand across his forehead, feeling for the first time the true gravity of the situation.

Sighing in agreement, Alto offered, "That won't do at all. What a pity the girl, imposter or no, had to show up now. Darwu was well on the way to becoming a suitable future king. His mate-less future had hardened his heart sufficiently. The years forged in battle had made him ruthless. He would have been better even than our own great father."

A sneer came across the king's face as he realized his brother would have liked nothing more than for Darwu not live up to their father's legacy. Alto probably wanted one of his sniveling sons to rule in Darwu's place. "Don't go counting the Crown Prince out as of yet. His future greatness is still very much within reach. All we need do is find a way to strategically dispose of the girl, whoever she is. If he feels betrayed by her, for example, he would surely feel the hatred and pain he needs to rule."

"Yes. Yes. I see now." Prince Alto nodded his head in agreement before halting suddenly. "But what if she is his mate and she becomes pregnant with the next heir to the throne before we can get rid of her?"

The king truly didn't know what to do should they be faced with such a dilemma. "Any heir could be a part of the very change she is prophesied to bring. And yet, this is an heir with our bloodline, our legacy as well. We need to get rid of her before any of that happens."

But he'd finally found his mate! That must have happened for a reason! The intrusion in his mind startled the king and he uttered a curse.

Woman! What have I told you about lurking? I am discussing things with Prince Alto that don't concern you.

If they concern my son, then they concern me. Did you see how happy he seemed this time? If the child survived the first death attempt on her life then your men bungled the chance. She is a woman now and they are mated. I suggest we approach the Cultide for help in containing whatever change she is destined to bring. The determination in Queen Hietha's voice indicated she had already made up her mind. She could never see reason when it came to her only child.

His heart softened momentarily, but the king knew he had to make the best decision for the monarchy, not for his mate's happiness. For the most part, his mate hardly ever questioned his decisions. But with their son, she took more liberties with her outspokenness than normal. And usually, he gave her some leeway. This time however, she needed to sit back and let him rule as he was meant to.

Trying to placate her, he murmured in her head, *You only want to do that so you can bounce any grandchildren she is destined to bring on your knees, My Mate.*

Is that so wrong? I am the Queen of Ourlane am I not? Why shouldn't I have my own little grandchildren? We were blessed only with Darwu and I went along with your decisions years ago because you convinced me the sacrifice was for the best. But if that young woman is indeed his mate, and I knew her saintly mother so trust me, the same aura of goodness and righteousness pulses from her skin. I don't know why the two of you are continuing to question this. And she will give me my grandchildren before you kill her. The whirlwind of words stormed his mind. Heitha surely would have been breathless had she been speaking aloud. That must be why women were not allowed to rule. Surely they would never be able to shut up long enough to do so.

His mate left his head, mentally turning her back on him and not speaking. The woman was truly too much. Too spoiled. Too much attitude. But she was his mate. The Queen of Ourlane, and he seldom denied her anything.

Chapter 9

Wake up, my darlings! You two didn't come to dinner last night. And your father was very disappointed, Darwu. But I assured him two newly mated young people have far better things to do than eat. At least I assumed that was the case since the servant said you hadn't touched the platter we sent up."

Kara looked up at the queen and then glanced over at the man whose arms curled around her as if they'd always belonged there. Had she slept the entire night nestled in Darwu arms like this? And why was the Queen of Ourlane fluttering around the room opening curtains and letting in dreaded sunshine?

The soft glow of the red sun beamed through the room and shed an awesome light on its contents. Too distracted by Darwu and his lovemaking, she hadn't really taken everything in the night before. The room, like every other part of the castle screamed wealth and prestige. Everything from the huge four-poster canopied bed they lay in to the rich silk drapes the queen opened busily, caused the pressing and uncomfortable feeling to bombard her chest again.

Darwu pulled Kara close and she could feel the distinct bulge pressing against her. Gritting her teeth and willing the sudden hardening of her nipples to stop, Kara tried unsuccessfully to block out the sudden smell of pine and desire attacking her nostrils. Her predicament would have been funny if it weren't so sad and weren't happening to her. Her body actually responded to his touch no matter what and no matter who was around. The queen was in the room for Divine's sake. Didn't the insatiable Warrior Prince ever take a break?

Insatiable. Now there's a word for it, because I certainly can't get enough of you. His hands slowly caressed her body under the blanket and she groaned as he found her nipples.

"Mother can you simply have the servants bring us up some breakfast and we will be down shortly, some time today, or this evening." Darwu spoke the words as he worked her nipples and squeezed her breast.

Kara stifled a sigh as she tried to maintain a façade of nonchalance.

The queen continued to flounce about fiddling with drapes and talking a mile a minute. "Well that won't do, Darwu. You have to meet with your father, uncle, and cousins. The king wants to hold council this morning. And our new princess has to be fitted for her new clothes."

"New clothes?" Springing up in bed and causing Darwu's grasping hands to fall away, Kara clasped the blanket to her naked body and peered at the queen.

"Why, yes, dear. Clothing befitting of a princess. You can't expect to wear those things you were wearing. You look more like a soldier than a princess in that get-up." The soft smirk briefly crossing the queen's lips gave Kara pause. What happened to the woman on the steps yesterday who couldn't stop proclaiming how beautiful Kara was?

"That's fine with me. I like clothing that protects from the elements one is liable to run into out in the bush," Kara protested.

"Well, you won't have to worry about being out in the bush anymore. You are a princess now. And a princess wears pretty gowns, spends her days sipping tea and entertaining, and her nights making future kings and queens so the current queen can have beautiful little ones to spoil," she gushed.

Kara almost snarled.

Turning a troubled gaze onto Darwu, Kara found him nodding his head in agreement with the Queen. *The rotten traitor.* Happy she had the small reprieve from his incessant mind prying, Kara thought both the prince and his mother were nuts if they thought she was going to parade around this evil castle in stupid fluffy gowns while the people of Ourlane suffered. She refused to be the cause of more suffering for the people.

"Oh, Your Highness, I'm truly fine with the clothing I have. I'm more comfortable in them. More importantly, well, I don't wear dresses. They don't look good on me at all." Kara tried to speak the words in a lighthearted manner but it was hard to do so between lips clenched tightly in a fake smile.

The queen gazed at her for a moment and then smiled her own false smile. "You are so much like your mother. She was a tree-climbing tomboy up until the time she found her true mate. But even *she* wore dresses. It's just more befitting of a lady, Kara. And remember everything you do now is a reflection of my son, the prince."

"Kara, it won't hurt you to humor my mother and let her help you get settled here." Darwu finally spoke and when he did, Kara wished he would shut up.

"Yes, that's exactly what I'm trying to do, son. And I am going to have my own personal seamstress, Donia work on this. She's the best. I'm so glad I got her out of that dreadful village before it was destroyed. She knew your mother as well. We were all girls together. Donia always had a talent with needle and thread. She made things for us most poor girls in our village could only dream about wearing. Knowing what she could do with so little, I knew I had to have her here. She is going to work wonders for our new princess." The Queen bounced about the room again chatting away.

Kara cringed at the hopelessness of trying to get the Queen of Ourlane to see anything other than her own point of view.

"That sounds fabulous, mother. But if you don't leave us to get ready for the day, then none of this will happen," Darwu offered suggestively.

"Oh, Darwu, darling, I'm so glad to have you back home. Do hurry and meet with your father and his council, so you can make some time to spend with your mother later." The queen rushed over and brushed her lips across Darwu's forehead. "I realize you are mated now, but a mother still needs to see her only son and know that he cares."

Goodness, this woman is a piece of work, Kara thought within the confines of the tiny, Darwu-free space in her mind. As small as that space was, it had become a much relished and coveted spot. She had to find room for expansion.

The queen left the room and Kara finally trusted herself to speak.

"Darwu, I can't wear dresses. You will have to do something to get the queen to see that I am just fine the way I am," Kara pleaded. Surely he could appreciate her uneasiness. He was a warrior. How would he feel if someone put him in a stupid frilly dress?

"No," Darwu responded a little too quickly for her taste.

"No?" Kara repeated the word between clenched teeth.

"No!" Darwu snapped.

How in all that was Divine was she expected to put up with a mate who so casually and callously disregarded her feelings?

"Oh, so that's it? I'm supposed to just take that? Your mother coming in here deciding to change my wardrobe and you deciding it's a good idea, while I apparently have no say?"

"Watch yourself, Kara. Need I remind you of how we punish mouthy mates? Did my warnings to you wear off already? Are you in need of a reminder? We don't have a lot of time, as I have to meet with my father and uncle, but I would be more than happy to take a moment to provide you with the correction you seem to need." The edge on Darwu's voice was all the threat she needed.

Kara didn't want to find herself spread over his lap getting spanked so soon after the last two. Her bottom was still sore and in the end, it would do no good. She was doomed by fate to be a stupid, dress-wearing princess. *Fine then*, she thought wearily. But, if Darwu got to be the much-feared Warrior Prince, then she saw no reason why she couldn't be the Warrior Princess. She would find ways to make her new station work for her, the people and the cause of The Resistance, or she would die trying.

"So we have decided to let the girl live for now, but also to keep her under close watch. If she—"

Darwu knew his decision was unprecedented and something he would have never even considered a few weeks ago, but he had to interrupt his father, the King of Ourlane. No way would he even allow thoughts of harming Kara to be spoken. "Of course she will live. No harm will *ever* come to my mate. If anyone so much as touches her, I won't be responsible for my actions."

The smirk crossing his cousin, Prince Gab's face made Darwu even angrier. Gab even let out a chuckle before pretending to placate him with, "Oh calm down, cousin. No one is going to hurt her, as long as she is who you claim she is, and she minds her place." The short, somewhat pudgy man had the same useless build as his father.

Darwu jumped up from his seat and walked over to Gab. He needed to make things very clear. No one was going to touch Kara, much less harm her in any way. He would kill them all first. Darwu was almost shocked by how vehemently he felt about this discussion or his cousin's off-handed remarks.

His other cousin, Prince Jorge, jumped up a second after Darwu did and leaped between Darwu and Gab. The muscular Jorge at least gave off a hint he might be able to handle himself in a battle. But Darwu knew from growing up with them both that wasn't the case. He could easily beat the two of them, had beaten the two of them, time and time again. Gab stood, staring at Darwu with a half smirk-half sneer plastered on his face. Darwu wanted to punch the snide expression off Gab's face but didn't in deference to his father and his uncle.

"Enough!" the King snapped, "Both of you sit down. We have enough going on without the two of you starting up."

Gab backed away and sat down followed by Jorge. Darwu took a deep breath vowing to take the matter up with his cousin later.

"Showing dissension in the monarchy, especially now that we finally have the rebel leadership of The Resistance behind bars, isn't very smart." Prince Alto shook his head in disappointment. "We need a strong show of unity at this time. We need to be on one accord when we put those traitors to death. Who knows how much of their misguided message has resonated with the peasants of Ourlane? If we handle this properly, we won't have to worry about others taking up their cause."

Darwu wondered how members of the same family, from the same bloodline could be so different. Where his uncle was short, fat and somewhat pathetic, his father was tall, strong, and powerful.

Nodding in agreement, the king added, "You're right, Alto. The way we handle this has strong implications for the future. That is why, we need to be sure that my son's new mate hasn't been too negatively influenced by the years she spent with her uncle and The Resistance."

"She has strong beliefs," Darwu said. "But I believe the longer we are mated and once we start our family, she will come to see the error of what she has been taught." He didn't want to disrespect his father, but he wasn't about to allow seeds to be sown that would put his mate in danger. "She is my mate and I take full responsibility for her. If she needs to be corrected, if she needs to be taught, if she needs to be punished, I will do so. I acknowledge you as the ruler of this land, father. And I respect you in every endeavor. But as your heir, I am asking that you grant me sovereignty when it comes to my mate. If we are to raise the future heirs of the monarchy, then we need to come to our understanding together. Just like you and my mother."

Surely his father would understand the way of Divine mates. Darwu knew the king struggled with the queen sometimes and therefore should at least be open enough to let Darwu tame Kara. All he needed was time to get her into shape, and time to wipe all thoughts of The Resistance clear from her mind.

The king narrowed his gaze and then turned to look out of the window for a moment.

"Nephew, this is a delicate matter. The king's relationship with your mother and your relationship, with this rabble-rouser are two different things—" Prince Alto hedged before being interrupted by the king.

"Fine, son. I grant you dominion in this matter and trust your judgment. But I want you to know that if things go awry, if she truly can't be trusted or proves to be a threat and not your sacred mate, then you'll both be punished accordingly. Is she worth your life, son?" Darwu knew his father was expecting him to back down.

Startled Darwu didn't even have to think about his response. "She is, Father. Now that I have found my mate, I realize I wouldn't want to live without her."

Prince Alto cleared his throat, while Jorge and Gab gave each other pointed stares. Darwu made sure to look each of them dead in the eye, before returning his gaze to his own father.

"Very well. I hope we will never have to ever act on this because it would break my heart. But I just wanted to be sure you understood the seriousness of this matter." The king stood. "We will set the execution of the five rebel leaders for five days hence. As Alto has mentioned, we need to take full advantage of this moment. We must strike fear in the hearts of all. The executions should be as horrific as we can make them, so the people will know not to test the crown ever again. These can't be the typical hangings. We need to make strong examples of these traitors."

"We could feed them to the lions. Have them cast into a cage so the people can watch them be devoured." Gab beady little eyes glowed with joy at the thought.

"That's a great idea. If a spectacle such as this doesn't still those bleeding hearts, I don't know what will," Jorge backed his brother's gruesome choice with glee.

"Normally, I don't go in for all the blood and gore. But, I think in this case, given the amount of years, time and energy the army put into finding these traitors, we need to make a strong statement." Their father, Prince Alto, nodded in agreement.

Darwu noticed they all stared at him, waiting for him to weigh in on what he felt the punishment should be. He couldn't believe that after all his years of fighting The Resistance he didn't want to contribute to how the leaders would meet their final deaths. The Resistance had after all taken care of his mate and kept her safe. They might have taught her useless and misguided philosophies, but she was alive because of them.

"Son," the king probed. "What do you think? How should The Resistance die?"

"Well, I don't know, father" Darwu answered truthfully.

"Well, you are the one who finally captured them, the one who spent the past five years tracking them down and killing them. Now that you've found the ringleaders, you have no thoughts on how they should die?" Gab's tone was disbelieving and he shook his head with skepticism.

"That's right, I don't," Darwu snapped as his lips turned into a sneer. Gab was going to be thrown out of a window if he didn't shut up. It was all Darwu could do to remain seated. "As you've noted, cousin, *I* was the one who hunted them down and brought in the monarchy's public enemy number one. The least you can do is think of a way to punish them now. I have to leave something for you to do or else what purpose would you serve."

"Enough!" The king snapped. "Darwu is right. He has captured our most wanted felons. Men who have broken every law in this land and whose punishment really doesn't need much discussion. In five days the rebels will meet their death in a display for all to see so the example won't be missed. No one will be allowed to go against the throne and live!" The king slammed his hand forcefully on the table.

Dawru cringed at his father's words. He hadn't missed any of the implied threats to himself and his mate. He made up his mind then and there to double, indeed triple his efforts to get Kara to see reason. She could not be allowed to harbor her treasonous thoughts any longer.

Chapter 10

Kara looked at the queen and her seamstress as if they both had lost their minds. *Dresses. No way.* She wouldn't be caught dead in a dress. She wasn't a stupid princess. She was a warrior, a warrior who wanted to cry. How had she gone from fighting in the bush for freedom to being confined by a life of frills and lace?

"You know, Donia, with her complexion, I can see her in beautiful bright pinks and oranges. What do you think?" The queen sat on a chair as Donia, the seamstress, measured Kara.

The petite and pretty woman with tightly coiled twists in her dark hair walked around Kara with her dreaded measuring tape and a mouth full of pins. The pensive expression on her face showed she was seriously considering the horrid colors the queen had mentioned.

Kara stared aimlessly into space wishing the floor beneath her would open up and swallow her. If the Divine truly hadn't forsaken her, then surely she would be able to just disappear and spare herself the fate awaiting her.

Ever since the two women came barging into the suite she shared with Darwu, Kara had been thinking the most wicked, disrespectful thoughts about the dress-happy queen. She kept them hidden in her new secret space. She was sure if Darwu knew half the things she was thinking about his mother, he would have come storming in to punish her by spanking her naked behind yet again.

A tingle went through her at the erotic memory of Darwu's first spanking, how it almost made her orgasm. Then the memory of the humiliation she felt with the second one, at being punished like a child, took all the sensuous feelings away. She was also certain about two other things: there would be *no more* spankings if she could help it, and she *wasn't* wearing anybody's *stupid* dress.

"I don't know, Your Highness," Donia replied after she removed the stickpins from her mouth, took a seat and picked up her sketchpad. As she gazed at Kara, she started to doodle. "I'm seeing her in nice rich earth tones, coppers, tans, taupes, browns."

"With lace?" The queen suggested more than asked.

"I'm thinking the princess should have her own style. Very much the way the gowns I design for you give you your own flair, Your Highness. The gowns I design for the lesser princesses, well, they tend to be standard fare. But as your son's sacred mate, this princess should stand out from all others with a style of her own. As the mate of the Warrior Prince, with some battle experience of her own, people will already be watching." Donia continued to doodle on her silly pad and Kara inwardly cringed.

Kara didn't want a *style*. She already had a *style*. It was no-maintenance-battle-ready, and she loved it.

"Keep talking, Donia." At the mention of Darwu, the queen seemed to bounce off her seat with interest. "You know I'm all for making my wonderful son shine. His mate is a reflection of him, and I want his future reign to be stellar. His legacy is mine you know."

Kara thought it strange the queen claimed Darwu's legacy as her own and left the king out of it. She decided the entire castle was weird and she would do well to just try and keep her wits about her so she didn't develop any of their abnormal tendencies as well.

"Well," Donia said as she showed the queen her sketchbook. "As you can see, the design is a mixture between formal and active. As a Warrior Princess, used to the bush, she needs a style that speaks to her uninhibited nature. This design is flexible, the half hoop skirt is detachable and will be made of a natural fiber, something earthy and durable, but also beautiful. Something people will be able to see, recognize, and perhaps relate to. I have been itching to work with some other fabrics."

Kara inched over to the two women and leaned over Donia's shoulder. While the drawing she saw was still a god-awful dress, it had a uniqueness that didn't seem to scream ruthless, bloodsucking, and money-grabbing royal. Plus, the half-skirt that wrapped around and spilt up the front revealed a nice pair of pants. It looked rather appealing actually. If in a hurry she could ditch the stupid half skirt and even if she had to keep it, the pants still allowed her to move with ease and comfort.

"I'm thinking the princess's gown should be designed using a mixture of the softest leathers, raw silk, and durable mud cloth. The pants here underneath would be made of leathers and mud cloth. The bodice, well, we can play with the design and have everything from dainty raw silk to a daring leather bustier," Donia half-mumbled as she continued to scribble.

The queen's eyes narrowed. "Are you sure we don't want to go with something a bit more traditional, Donia. She is still a princess. Shouldn't she at least have some frill and lace in there some where?"

No. No. Hell no! Kara chanted in her head. She was so caught up in the dialogue between the queen and Donia she forgot to keep her thoughts in her secret place.

What's wrong, Kara? Darwu's voice in her head startled her. What did he do, just lurk there until she had a thought and then pounced on it? Didn't he have more important things to do in the castle?

Nothing is more important to me than you, my mate. So tell me what is wrong.

I'm just here with the queen and her seamstress, Donia. They are coming up with my new style as mate to the Warrior Prince. A Warrior Princess.

A Warrior Princess? Darwu's voice chuckled in her head and Kara decided she didn't like his tone at all.

Yes, a Warrior Princess! Do you think you are the only one with battle experience? I am a warrior in my own right. And I should have a style that befits a woman of my stature. Kara fought the urge to stomp her feet as she thought the words. Slowly she let herself slip back into her secret place so as not to alert Darwu.

Oh come on, Kara, don't go all silent on me again. I miss your thoughts.

I'm busy, Darwu. I need to be at full attention here before your mother and her designer turn me into a powder princess with frills and lace.

Well, I'm en route to the suite and I think I'll add my input as well. I'd like to see you in some lace.

Kara focused on the Donia's doodling hand and tuned out Darwu. The woman had added in some lace to the sketch. *Why? By all that is Divine! Why?*

"I don't think we'd want to have too much lace. The image we are going for here is that of a woman who is worthy of a dynamic and strong man such as your son, the Warrior Prince," Donia said, stroking the queen's ego smoothly. "So I'll add dyed pieces of lace to the edges of some of the bodices, maybe an occasional strip can line the half skirts, especially when we are going with the raw silk. But this is not a lace princess. This is a leather princess."

A *leather princess.* Kara thought she rather liked the sound of that. It conjured all sorts of naughty images in her head along with flashes of power. Kara let out a breath she hadn't been aware she was holding. The lace didn't look that bad.

"So, what will our newest and most beautiful princess be wearing this season?" Darwu's loud voice barreled through the suite as he made his way towards them.

Kara turned and couldn't help but stare. The well-defined muscled on his sculpted chest almost seemed to beckon her to touch him. He still wore his leather pants, but his leather tunic had been exchanged for a lighter shirt of what appeared to be silk. But the soft fabric didn't take away from his masculinity. Indeed, the way the fabric clung to every rip and bulge of his muscles seemed to enhance his manly appeal.

Darwu walked over and stood behind Kara, pulling her in a tight embrace. Her breath caught and she swallowed several times to contain the sudden dryness in her throat.

The queen smiled as she pointed at Donia's design. "Donia has really outdone herself with this design, son. Your mate is going to shine and all of Ourlane will be whispering about Darwu, the Warrior Prince's new mate."

Kara gritted her teeth and willed her thoughts to remain cloaked. The queen's references to her as some sort of appendage or fashion accessory to the prince were getting on Kara's nerves and pushing her to the point of explosion.

She realized her first impression of how the Queen seemed to be the perfect companion to the king had been inaccurate. A future as a simple aside, an afterthought to a powerful man wasn't really her fate. Kara tried to imagine other alternatives. She had to make sure she kept her own mind and will.

Darwu pulled Kara close, his hands roaming her body as he studied the drawing. Each place his hands touched sent rivers of shock waves over her skin. The rivers all led to one place and that place left her soaking between her legs.

Not able to understand the automatic physical reaction and a little shamed by it, Kara gritted her teeth even more. Not only was the queen referring to her in a way that bothered her, but Darwu's possessive grip was starting to annoy her as well. Did he really have a right to just walk into a room and start pawing her? Even though his touch excited her to no end and moved her deep in her core, she was not his property.

Kara tried to move away from Darwu but he held her firmly. His hands rested on her hips when he was done caressing her thighs and behind. Kara hissed and grudgingly settled into his hold.

"I like it. the style is a bit untraditional. But does seem to fit Kara's spirit very well. Will each dress be different? What colors will they be?" Darwu's interest in fashion almost made Kara laugh out loud. He seemed more interested in the stupid dresses than she was.

Who would have thought the Warrior Prince contained such a sense of fashion?

The only thing she was concerned with was not looking like some freaky powder-princess with embellishments and lace. She could care less about the colors and the rest.

"I'm thinking earthy colors, brown, rust, copper, lots of copper actually. It would bring out her coloring well. And the slight copper flecks in her eyes." Donia looked up from her sketch and into Kara's eyes. For a brief moment Kara thought she might actually have an ally, maybe even a friend in the castle, but Donia quickly diverted her gaze back to her sketches.

Darwu used his hold on Kara to physically turn her around to face him. Kara glanced up at him and her heart skipped. He gazed deep into her eyes, studying her intently and making her melt. Kara took a deep breath.

Darwu was the first to blink and break the lock between their stare. "You're right, Donia. She does have copper flecks in her eyes." He stared at Kara again and she swallowed. "You have beautiful eyes."

The queen cleared her throat. "Well, I can see the two of you need to be left alone. Come, Donia, I'm sure you want to get started on your new designs and I'm sure Kara can't wait to wear them." The queen paused as she walked out of the room and turned to Kara. "I will have one of the servants bring you a few of Gab's mate, Seake's dresses, to borrow until yours are finished. You will need something appropriate to wear to dinner and on other occasions."

The image of the frilly gowns she knew those sniveling princesses wore came into Kara's mind. "Actually, Your Highness, I can wear my own clothing until Donia is finished."

"That won't do at all dear. To be quite frank, your clothing is horrid and not befitting of any woman, let alone a princess." The queen shook her head in disgust and Kara wished she could smack the woman.

Just one smack, Divine, just one!

"I can work on this all night and have at least one of your gowns ready for you in the morning, Princess Kara," Donia offered.

An overwhelming sense of guilt came over Kara at Donia's words. She did not want the woman to stay up all night making a dress for her. Was she so quickly becoming one of the royals that she would have a woman deprive herself of sleep just so she could have a dress? *No way.*

"That's okay, Donia, don't trouble yourself," Kara mumbled softly. If she had to, she would wear the stupid dresses.

"It's no trouble. It's her job," The queen snapped.

"I said that's okay." Kara turned to the queen and forced a smile. "I will borrow Princess Seake's gowns until mine are finished. There is no rush." Kara turned back to Donia and spoke firmly.

"Well, that's settled. We'll see you at dinner, mother," Darwu pointed glanced toward the exit showed his lack of subtlety.

"Oh, you want to be alone with your mate to get started on my grandbabies. Wonderful!" Gushing, the queen stood and headed towards the door.

Kara let out her breath as the two women left the room. What she had come to recognize as Darwu's mating scent wafted through the air and her resistance began to slowly chip away.

Darwu bent his head and captured her mouth in a kiss. She allowed the slow seductive travels of his tongue to lure her momentarily. His lips, soft but firm, gave her a sense of pleasure unlike anything she'd ever experienced. She was sure his kisses could teach her a whole new meaning of surrender.

She hesitantly broke away and gazed up at him. The emotion she saw evidenced in his eyes took her breath away. She had seen the special bond between other sacred mates but she didn't understand the intensity of the bond. Looking at it from the outside was entirely different from being entrenched in it. Every tender glance, every soft caress, every heartfelt desire doubled back and multiplied between the two of them until she couldn't distinguish her growing feelings from his. She swallowed and closed her eyes.

"Why am I feeling like you are pulling away from me? As if you are holding something back? But that can't be because I know your heart and mind. I still can't help feeling like something is wrong." Darwu pondered as his hand traced her face looking for clues.

"I don't know why you're feeling that way, Darwu. We both know I can't pull away from you, that I'm stuck to you for the rest of our lives." Kara knew her voice sounded gloomier than she actually felt and was surprised. When had she become resigned, even a little bit happy, to be linked to the Warrior Prince?

"You say that as if it's a death sentence or a prison term. Most people would be happy that they'd found their other half." She could see her words had wounded him, but she had to keep him away from the questions he was starting to ask. He couldn't know her secret. He was better off worrying about other things.

"We aren't most people, are we? You can't tell me you are happier about me being your sacred mate than I am at you being mine. I'm connected to you. I know you are the only one for me. I crave your touch more than anything I've ever desired in the world. I feel my heart opening to you more and more each day and softening in love and devotion, which can't be helped because of who I am to you. I am yours, Darwu. But I don't have to like it." Kara bit out the words harshly and was surprised by the feeling of her own heart breaking a bit.

"Oh, but that's where you're wrong, my mate. You do have to like it. My heart can't take any misery on your part, especially if you are miserable about our sacred connection." Pausing a moment, Darwu simply stared at her before continuing. "Even though, I may not have wanted a rebel as my sacred mate, the Divine has sanctioned our union. And I will never give you up. You are mine so you might as well get used to it and become happy about it. We have a very long time to be together, Kara."

"This is crazy, Darwu. I really shouldn't be here. I'm not supposed to be here. The only thing that feels right is you, us. How can that be?" Kara pulled away and sat on the bed. She tried to shake off the overwhelming presence of guilt threatening to overcome her. She couldn't believe she felt so bad about keeping her thoughts secret from Darwu. She had asked him to give her room and to get out of her head. She needed time to get used to their connection. He was such a force that she had to spirit away a small space for herself or he would overtake every single piece of her and nothing would be left.

"If it feels right, why do you fight so hard?" Sitting down beside her on the bed, he wrapped his arm around her and pulled her close. She shut her eyes and buried her head in his chest, allowing herself to feel his heartbeat and be calmed by the strong, steady pulse of him. Every thump echoed his care.

"How was the meeting today? Did the king decide what he—" Even though she didn't really want to know what the king had decided to do with her uncle and the others, she had to ask. Before she could finish asking, Darwu cut her off.

He let out a hiss. "Kara, darling, please don't bring this up now."

"But I want to know what will happen to my uncle and the others. Perhaps the king could find it in his heart to be lenient to them as a show of good faith to the people of the land. They are the people that The Resistance has fought for all these years. Perhaps if the king could see his way clear to—"

"Kara, stop it. Stop it now! Your uncle and the other traitors to the throne will be killed in five days. They will meet the harshest punishment imaginable and will be examples to all others of what happens when you go against the throne." Darwu got up from the bed and paced the floor. "I know you think you need to remain loyal to that band of lying traitors, but from this point on, your only loyalty is to me, your mate. If you do not find a way to reconcile yourself to your fate then you put both our lives in danger, because my father will surely kill anyone who resists his power. Since I could never allow anyone to take you away from me, he'd have to kill me too." His eyes narrowed. "Is that what you want? Do you want us both to die because you can't seem to back away from your irrational attachments to The Resistance?"

"Irrational!"

"Yes, irrational! They make no sense, Kara, none at all. You will stop it now." He pulled her up from the bed in a tight embrace and his lips connected harshly with her own.

A stifled moan escaped her mouth as his tongue cleared a path past her teeth. The blur of touching and groping left her standing naked before him, caught her by surprise, but she had no time to react. She was on her back, across the bed and responding to his touch.

Blinking rapidly she murmured, "Darwu, we need to talk about this. We need to come to—" Before she could finish her words Darwu had disrobed and hilted himself deep inside her. She gasped at the sudden intrusion and shut her eyes tightly.

Princess. Princess Kara. The future Queen of Ourlane. My sacred mate. My one heart's desire. I need to know you are mine and only mine. You have to break your ties to The Resistance. You have to.

I'm not a Princess, Darwu. I'm truly not. I would never be happy sitting on my butt while the people of Ourlane suffer. Kara didn't bother to fight against the thrust of his hips but instead met his with her own. The feeling of him inside of her had a dizzying effect.

Kara, I don't want to punish you in order to help you to see the error of your ways. But I will if necessary. I will do whatever I must to make you understand you belong to me. We belong together. Your life with The Resistance is behind you and The Resistance is dead. Each word was punctuated with powerful thrusts.

Never as long as I draw breath. Kara felt a sharp stab of pain in her heart as soon as she thought the words. The pain transferred from Darwu's heart to hers in awful, unbearable waves. She couldn't stand it. Moving into the secret spot in her head, she tried to find some peace from the pain she was causing her mate. She found none. His heartache was hers and vice versa.

She closed her eyes and willed her secret space to get bigger. *Please, by all that is Divine, shield me. Cloak me. Protect me. Cover me.* She felt safe from his prying, but she still felt his broken heart.

Reaching out physically, she touched his heart and tried to heal the ache so they might both find some rest. As she touched his heart with their hips thrusting in a furious mating, she knew she had never felt closer and more connected to anyone in her life. As he marked her as his in the oldest of ways, she wrapped her heart and her mind around him unbeknownst to him.

She saw the love. The prince had really come to love her. He'd loved her for a long time. He'd loved the little girl he couldn't save. She wondered if she had been a little older would she have learned to live with the pain of losing him as Darwu had lived with the pain of losing her?

Closing her eyes and willing him peace she poured her love over him like a balm. Every place in him where she found darkness or sadness, she covered with love. The guilt he'd felt at not being able to save her that once threatened to engulf him, was pierced with her healing heart. Her soothing spirit quieted the anger and helplessness Darwu felt because of his father's threats. Her every thought and desire became focused on helping and healing him.

Do you feel that, Kara? Our love is so strong. We can't allow anything to come between what the Divine has brought together. Tell me you feel it. Darwu thrust his hips furiously. He went deeper inside her when she hadn't thought he could.

I feel it. I do. Kara allowed herself to feel the radiant happiness coming from her mate. Each stroke sent her closer and closer to the point of near extinction. She swore she was going to explode from pleasure and disappear.

His lips locked onto hers and his tongue penetrated her mouth in the same fashion his penis rocked her core. She felt a tightening in her gut and she almost lost the hold she had on his heart and mind. She didn't want to lose the connection because she realized it was special. She held on tightly as her orgasm ripped through her.

Ahh, Kara, I love the way you tighten around me when you come. It makes it so hard to not come myself. But I have to hold on because I need to feel your sex tightening around me at least twice more before I find release. Darwu made the wicked promise and her eyes glazed.

Twice more? Kara thought as she slowly drifted back down to earth. Surely, he didn't really mean to have her orgasm twice more. She wouldn't survive it.

True to his word he brought her to release twice more before spilling his seed deep inside of her. His mouth covered hers in a stirring kiss that seemed to draw her out of herself and into him. She felt their souls connect and she wasn't sure where he ended and she began.

The melding was so complete it shocked her at first. She could feel his strength, the goodness in his heart, the rage that used to motivate him, which was slowly ebbing away, and being replaced by love; love for her. He wrapped his arms around her and she relished the feelings bouncing off him. The warmth of his hold sent tingles across her body. He stroked her hair and kissed her face gently.

I've got to find a way to get her to accept her fate. If only she weren't such a spirited and willful woman. I can't lose her. And if she doesn't stop this nonsense about The Resistance, she'll be risking her life. I have to find a way to make her see the error of her ways. Darwu thought this all while kissing and holding her.

All she could do was remain quiet and cloaked. Being able to hear his thoughts shocked her. She knew they had connected in a way they hadn't before and she could feel him in new and powerful ways, but didn't think she could also know his thoughts.

He had some nerve. He was still plotting to bend her to his will, even when he held her in his arms so sweetly.

Soon, the leaders of The Resistance will be dead and then maybe she'll see that no good can come from treason. Until then, I'll just love her and hope for an heir. Once she is pregnant and has the responsibility of raising our children, she'll have other things to occupy her mind.

Darwu's mouth covered hers and she kissed him back, all the while trying to cloak her broken heart. She knew any pain she felt would cause him pain and his pain would impact her. If nothing else, she just needed a moment of reprieve from the pain that had become their relationship.

"What's wrong?" Darwu asked.

"Nothing" Kara mumbled.

"You don't seem to be thinking anything? Why is that? I miss the feel of your thoughts," Darwu said as he snuggled with her.

Since he still seemed to be thinking thoughts of how to bend her to his way, she had a hard time reconciling his actions with his will.

"I know my thoughts upset you. So I've been censoring them to keep you from being angry," Kara offered half-truthfully knowing if he saw all she'd been thinking and all she'd been hiding, anger wouldn't come close to describing what he'd feel.

Darwu expelled a hiss of breath and closed his eyes for moment. "I feel a sadness coming from you I wish wasn't there."

"I can't help it, Darwu. You have to realize how very hard this is for me. I'm in a place where I don't know anyone and all the people I know and love are about to be killed. Tell me, how can I not be sad?" Kara voice choked and she quickly turned her face into her pillow. She had no desire to start crying in front of Darwu. He was busy plotting her fall, she didn't want him to see how broken she'd become.

Please don't be sad, my mate. Please. Darwu spoke the words in her mind in a soft pleading whisper.

I will try was all she could think back without bursting into a tirade and exposing all she now knew to him. She vowed she would find a way to stop the execution of her uncle and the rest of The Resistance. She was also going to make her mate see she had a mind and ideas of her own and she refused to let them go. He would either learn to live with her as she was or they would both be miserable for the rest of their mated lives.

Chapter 11

Darwu held his mate hoping she would finally see the light. She was no longer going on and on about The Resistance. Even her thoughts seemed more resigned to her life as it now was. She said she was tempering her thoughts so she wouldn't upset him. He supposed it was as good a start.

The knock on the door to their quarters pulled him from his contemplative state.

His mother entered the suite without waiting for an invite. "Hello, darlings. I wanted to bring Princess Kara, one of the dresses from the lesser princesses to wear for dinner tonight. More will be brought to her shortly so she will have suitable clothing until Donia finishes the special designs." The queen held a frilled lace frock with pink ribbons in front of her.

Darwu braced himself for the outrage, Kara would undoubtedly express. He couldn't imagine his mate willingly wearing such overly frilly attire and he knew he would have to convince her otherwise. His mother was right after all. The subjects of Ourlane would expect the Prince's mate be dressed accordingly.

He watched Kara as she stared at the dress. She didn't say anything and she didn't seem to be thinking anything either. *Odd.*

"I can see the two of you are busy." The queen said. "Just don't be late for dinner. Your father was upset last night when you missed dinner. We need to have a formal meal to welcome you home, son." The queen headed toward the door and turned before leaving. "Oh, and to celebrate your new mate."

"Yes, Mother. We will be down shortly." As soon as the Queen left he turned Kara to face him. "Okay, Kara, I know you have something to say about the dress. I know you don't want to wear it."

"How do you know, Darwu? And if so, do you care?" Kara's blank expression and detached demeanor didn't match the words she spoke.

He sputtered for a moment, tongue-tied as he tried to think of an answer to her question. "That's not the point, Kara."

Kara got up from the bed. His eyes followed the long lean stretch of her seductive body as she walked away from the bed, grabbing the dress and taking it with her.

"Where are you going?"

Only a slight change in the timbre of her voice and the barely noticeable slouch in her shoulders showed something deeper was wrong with his mate. Darwu wanted to get to the bottom of things immediately.

Briefly turning, Kara replied, "I'm taking this Divinely awful dress and getting ready for this dinner because I know you could really care less what I think or feel and frankly it sickens me to be around you right now."

"Kara, don't just walk away," Darwu snapped.

She didn't even bother to look back and continued into the adjoining room. Darwu narrowed his eyes as he tried to figure out exactly what happened. One minute they had been making love and he'd felt an intense connection to her. Then, just like that, the connection was gone. He tried to probe her mind to see if he could figure out exactly what had happened.

Besides stray thoughts about how much she hated the dress, he couldn't gauge a thing. She seemed fine. Just irritated at wearing the dress. He sensed something deeper and more profound was bothering her. Darwu threw on his clothing and walked into the back room where Kara was dressing.

She turned when he entered and he had to inhale in order not to lose his breath. His mate was beautiful.

"I know it looks horrid doesn't it?" Kara glanced down at the dress and frowned.

"No, far from it. I—you—I—well I've never seen a more gorgeous woman in all my life. You were captivating in your leather pants and tunic. Now you are breathtaking. Divine help me when Donia makes those seductive gowns she has in mind." He was head over heels in love with his mate and falling further every minute.

How would he ever be able to deny her anything? But how could he not deny her when the one thing she seemed to want the most would be the equivalent of signing both their death warrants?

Darwu frowned as frustration started to overwhelm him. He couldn't take the chance his father wouldn't have her killed if she continued advocating for The Resistance.

If his father killed Kara, he would have to kill Darwu too, because Darwu knew in the depth of his soul if anyone harmed her, he would kill them or die trying.

The realization that his thoughts were now bordering on treason was not lost on him. What were they going to do?

He glanced at Kara and found her studying him intently. She walked over to him and wrapped her arms around him. The very act alone removed any remaining coldness in his heart.

The warrior had softened at the touch of a woman.

Willow, rose, desire, and seduction wafted through the air as she stood on her tiptoes and planted a soft loving kiss on his lips. His spirit shifted. All his worries about his father and The Resistance faded into the background and all he could feel was the warmth and love coming from his mate.

How could her touch have the power to calm him, to heal him?

"We'd better go, Darwu. We don't want to miss dinner again. I think the queen would surely have a fit if we did." A sweet smile crossed her lips as she slowly pulled away from their embrace.

Pausing for a moment to contemplate if they could indeed get away with not going to dinner, Darwu decided to make a quick appearance at dinner and then return to his quarters with his mate.

Planting one more kiss on her lips, he sighed and enclosed her hand in his. "You're right, Kara. We should be on our way. If we spend another moment here, we won't make dinner."

She glanced down at her dress, sighed and walked out of the room.

As they traveled down the halls of the castle, he watched the gentle sway of her hips and fought not to turn around and take her back to his suite.

When they entered the formal dining room, everyone was already seated. His cousins and their wives, his uncle and his wife, as well as his parents, the King and Queen of Ourlane waited for them.

The queen smiled brightly. "I told you they would make it tonight."

Eyes narrowed in annoyance, the king snapped, "Yes, well, it's about time."

"Oh we know how it is with new mates, especially when you get one as hot as that wench." Gab leered at Kara before turning to his own wife. "That dress never looked as good on you, Seake. You might as well give it to the new High Princess permanently."

Darwu narrowed his gaze on his cousin and knew that if the fool wasn't careful, he would be forced to kill him that very night.

"Oh look at his face. I'd watch myself, brother." Jorge offered a jovial laugh but Darwu could see the menace behind it. "We all know how the *Warrior* Prince gets when we talk about his new mate."

"Come on, let's not tease Prince Darwu." Alto got up and walked over to Kara and Darwu. "Welcome to the castle, princess. We're very happy the Crown Prince has found his sacred mate." Alto embraced Kara and Darwu felt a jolt of energy come from Kara that sent shockwaves through him.

Dawru stared at Kara and noticed she was breathing irregularly and had taken several steps back. She wrapped her arms around herself and seemed to be looking for a way out of the room.

Doing a quick search of her mind, he tried to see what had caused her to react so strongly. He couldn't find anything. *What's wrong, Kara?*

Kara's eyes widened and she turned. *Nothing. Nothing is wrong.*

Something is wrong. What I want to know is why are you hiding things from me. Better yet, how are you hiding things from me?

Kara plastered a smile on her face and eyed the rest of the people in the room. She wouldn't look at him at all. *I'm not hiding anything. Let's just sit down and get this crazy dinner over and done with so that I can get out of this foolish dress.*

The image of helping her out of her dress overcame him and he lost his train of thought.

Kara turned to Alto with the same fake smile on her face. "Thank you for your warm welcome, Prince Alto. I'm very happy that Darwu and I have been able to find one another. I didn't think I would ever find my other half." Kara stepped to the side and moved towards the table.

Darwu watched his uncle's face and didn't appreciate the suspicious way the man observed Kara. He especially didn't like the glance that passed between his uncle and his father.

Kara sat down at the long elegant dining table and tried to get her pulse under control. She had always thought Prince Alto and his sons, Prince Jorge and Gab, were pure evil based on the role they played in collecting the enormous taxes from the people of Ourlane.

Meeting the men in person, being able to touch and feel their evilness first-hand, disturbed her more than she could have ever envisioned.

When Prince Alto had embraced her, she felt as if a cloak of evil attempted to penetrate her. The awful pressing came back and made her chest feel as though it were caving in. She had thought having Darwu in her mind was invasive. Having Alto try and break through her defenses was worse.

Her heart pounded and her stomach felt as if it were in battle. It was all she could do to hold herself together so Darwu didn't figure out what she was thinking or worse, discover she could read his mind and thoughts.

She felt horrible about not sharing her new connection to Darwu with him. But she needed to be able to use what she knew in order to save her Uncle Rafe and the rest of The Resistance. She reasoned that Darwu used information he stole from her head in order to capture The Resistance leaders, so she would use what she stole from him to set them free.

Turning to Darwu, she plastered another smile on her face. He seemed troubled and she already knew from studying his mind she needed to put up the best front possible. The king would waste no time having her killed, whether she was Darwu's mate or not. The vibes of harm and danger she got from Prince Alto let her know that she needed to fake her happiness and not give them any cause to kill her before she could save the others.

"So, Princess Kara," said Jorge's wife, Lara, "we hear you were a member of those awful rebels, The Resistance. Did you actually live in the bush and fight battles?" The petite woman wore an elaborate hairstyle of tiny braids all twisted into a bun. Her bright, light-brown eyes flashed with interest.

Life as a princess must be hideously boring Kara thought and found she didn't blame the woman one bit for wanting to know something about life in the world outside the dreadful castle. She'd only been there two days and she already felt as though the walls were caving in around her.

"Yes, I did." Smiling, Kara didn't see any reason to lie. The king and his brother knew who she was and where she came from. If she tried to lie now, she would just send up a flag warning them to watch her more carefully.

"Well, let's not talk about this unpleasant business at dinner." The queen waved her hand in a dismissive manner at Lara and Kara both. "We are celebrating the return of my gorgeous and brave son, Darwu the Warrior Prince. Oh, and his newfound mate, the woman who is going to give me my grandchildren, the future heirs to the throne. All this rebel resistance business is irrelevant."

Kara noted the queen again saw her as an afterthought, an aside, and a brood mare. At that moment, she decided she couldn't control the way the queen viewed her, but she could control her own fate and her own destiny.

"It's irrelevant only if she is indeed done with her alliance to them." The king's eyes showed he no more believed her ability to change than he believed the hazy purple sky of Ourlane was blue.

Kara felt her skin crawl. The queen's misguided hold on Kara's ovaries gave her pause. Between the king's suspiciousness and the eerie evil vibes she felt from Prince Alto, she didn't know what to do. By all that was Divine did she have to find a way to deal with all the crazy royals and Darwu too? The task was bigger than any one woman, warrior or not, could bear.

Are you okay? Darwu's deep voice echoed in her head and she looked up.

I'm fine. Kara tried to place a pleasant expression on her face. Even though the food in front of her smelled heavenly, she had no appetite.

"Are you, Princess Kara?" Alto's fat smarmy face and beady eyes seemed stuck on her for some reason.

Kara didn't know what Prince Alto was talking about. Juggling the secret thoughts in her head, Darwu's constant presence and the outer conversations going on around her, quickly became a chore. "Am I what?"

Shaking his head in annoyance Prince Alto hissed, "Done with your alliance to The Resistance?"

"If The Resistance is no more, then how can I be allied with them?" Answering a question with a question was one way around telling them how she really felt.

"True. But that doesn't really answer the question." The king clearly didn't buy her response.

Trying not to narrow her eyes and attempting to temper her response, Kara took on as diplomatic a tone as she possibly could given the sudden inquisition. "I don't know what else I could possibly say. Nothing is left for me to be allied with. You have the leaders of The Resistance locked up and they will be executed soon."

"I'm troubled by your lack of response, princess." Alto tsked and threw his napkin down on the table.

"Oh really, enough of this! The Resistance is no more. The future of the monarchy is what is important and this girl—our son's mate—is crucial to that." The queen spared Kara a glance and seemed to roll her eyes as well. "Let us dwell on that, the future, my grandchildren, and move on."

The king narrowed his gaze on his wife. "Fine, we will discuss it after dinner in my chambers."

The queen turned and gave the king an angry glare and he closed his eyes for a moment. The entire table went silent as if they could eavesdrop on what was going on inside the king and queen's heads.

Kara had a feeling the queen was sharing some less than pleasant words telepathically with her mate. From the expression of anger and the slow resignation crossing his face, Kara figured they wouldn't be asked to go to the king's quarters after dinner.

After less than two minutes, the queen's face broke out into a bright beam and she turned to Darwu. "Don't worry about your father's harsh words, my beautiful son. He just worries unnecessarily." The queen turned to Kara, and while her face still held a smile, the pleasant happiness seemed to disappear. Her eyes appeared hollow and vacant. "I know my son's mate would do nothing to harm him." The words were spoken more like a warning.

Kara realized that although the queen pretended to be an ally, she probably should be watched *more* than the others. The woman had an agenda and that was the only reason Kara was still alive.

As Kara tried to figure out why the queen wanted to keep her alive, she plastered a smile on her own face. "Of course I would never do anything to put my mate at harm. To do so would be the equivalent of breaking my own heart." The truth of the words struck her startling her.

Turning to face Darwu, she found him searching her with the same puzzled gaze he'd been wearing from the moment she figured out how to keep parts of her thoughts hidden. Even though she had started to filter meaningless thoughts in her head, he still seemed suspicious.

Smiling at her mate, she finished her dinner and prayed the Divine would allow her to rescue her uncle and the others without getting herself and Darwu killed.

Chapter 12

What are you doing? Donia smiled when she heard the words of her mate in her head. As she sat alone in her chambers busily sewing Kara's clothing, she'd also been thinking about Rafe, wanting desperately to see him again.

Many times she had pitied herself and thought about how unfair life had been to her. She had been forced to give up her mate and her child when she was still too young to really know what having a mate meant.

She and Rafe had grown up together and had known they belonged to one another early in their lives. When Rafe's mother, also a powerful shamaness, told them of their destinies before she died, Donia wanted to run away from it all. She only wanted Rafe. She only wanted to raise her baby boy. But instead, she had to live in an evil castle and serve a childhood friend she barely recognized anymore.

Hietha, the Queen of Ourlane, had become a vain, power-hungry shrew of a woman.

It's no use thinking about how things might have been, love. Think of the wonderful future our son and his children will have if Kara is successful in fulfilling her destiny. She's going to need all the help she can get. Rafe's strong and reassuring words sent tremors of happiness through her.

Donia smiled because she liked Kara a lot. The young girl reminded her so much of Rafe's sister and even the young Hietha. They had all been shamanesses. Hietha just refused to use her power for good and allowed her power and herself to be corrupted.

Kara wasn't yet aware of the power she held.

I'm making her some gowns. Hietha is worried about Kara ruining the prince's image and wants her dressed as a proper princess.

A proper princess? My niece? Oh, Divine, Kara must be fuming. Please tell me you aren't making some frilly frock for the girl. She'd sooner die than wear it. Then we'd surely be doing this all for naught.

Oh, I have worked magic. And Kara, the Warrior Princess, will have clothing she can move around in, even battle in if need be. She will be the perfect match for the Warrior Prince.

Good. Now enough of them, my mate. Take a break from your task and tell me. What are you wearing?

A shiver went down Donia's back and goosebumps popped up all over her arms and neck as Rafe's words caressed her.

Rafe, I've missed you so much.

I've missed you too. Close your eyes, my heart, let me show you how much.

Donia closed her eyes and let her spirit connect with Rafe's. The images he painted of them together were far more vivid than anything he'd ever sent her when he was in the bush fighting with The Resistance. She could see his strong strapping body and his black curls slicked on his head from the sweat of their lovemaking. The vision of his dark eyes, hooded with passion, pierced her mind and her heart.

Having him so near caused such a stir in her emotions and her senses. She thought she could almost smell his scent of hibiscus, mango, and desire, always desire. She didn't know if it was his nearness in the castle, or her memories playing tricks on her, but controlling her need to run down to the dungeon and mate with him was the hardest thing she'd ever done.

She should have been happy that they could share these final moments together, but she couldn't help but think of the reason why he was so close. She was about to lose her life mate and she could do nothing to stop it.

Shh. Donia, my love, please let's enjoy the time we have together and let me show you how much I love you.

But Rafe, I don't think I can live without you. A tear slid down her cheek, slipping through her closed eyes.

The wonderful thing about Divinely inspired love is that it never dies. Our souls belong together and they will meet again. We are destined.

Donia felt the soft, tender touch of her mate as the images of him loving her body manifested in a swarm of sensations that threatened to explode in her. Just as she felt her body give into the intensity of her mate's mental loving, she felt his physic penetration stronger than she had ever felt it. The only time it had ever been stronger was when he actually held her in his arms.

Fully clothed and sitting at her sewing table, she felt naked. She felt as if she were beneath Rafe, him thrusting in and out of her at a vigorous pace. And it gave her a sense of peace and fulfillment.

Short panting breaths escaped her lips just as she felt the urgent probe of his powerful mouth on hers. He completed her as always, filling her with an abundance of pleasure and joy.

Ra—fe, Donia murmured softly. Seductive chills trailed her skin, leaving goose bumps in their path.

Shh. Donia just let me love you.

Throwing her head back, she let out a soft sigh as what was sure to be the first of many orgasms that evening trailed through her.

Once back in their quarters, Darwu tried to keep his emotions and his hormones at bay long enough to figure out just what wrong with Kara. Something was missing. He felt it just as surely as he felt his desire and love for her.

Reaching out he touched her face and closed his eyes. He let his mind merge deeply with hers and probed every nook of her brain. Yet he knew she was hiding something.

"I have to get out of this dress. I hate it. I can't believe I made it through the night dressed in this silly frock." Kara walked toward the connecting dressing room.

Darwu held her arm, caressing it as he spoke. "Allow me." He undid the many buttons on the dress and let the lacy garment fall to the floor. Seeing her beautiful body, he momentarily forgot any suspicions he had about her.

She nibbled her lips and raised her eyes to him. Stepping away from the puddle of the dress, she bent and took the delicate slippers from her feet.

Quickly removing his own clothing, Darwu lifted Kara in his arms and tried to make it to the bed before sliding into her heated womanhood. He tried, but the best he could do was to prop her up against the closed door to their quarters as he leaned further into her soft heat.

Kara brought her mouth down and kissed him. Darwu could feel the love exploding from her lips to his. The touch warmed his heart and pulsed joy through him unlike anything he'd ever experienced.

"Ummmm . . . Darwu . . .." Kara moaned from deep in her gut as she met his thrusts with her own.

Darwu groaned at the feel of her legs and arms wrapped around him, clutching him as her sex tightened around his.

Sticking his tongue deep in her mouth, he mimicked the movement of his hips, fast, sharp, hard, swift. When they were connected in their passion nothing else mattered.

Feeling the need to express exactly how he felt, Darwu halted his kiss and gazed deeply into Kara's eyes. Seeing his love mirrored there made his heart skip.

Tilting her head forward and smiling gently, Kara rolled her hips in a sweet seductive motion.

What are you doing to me? Lost in passion for a moment, Darwu wondered if it was really possible to feel such splendor.

He would have missed out on the feeling had she not turned up at his campsite. And he could lose the feeling if he didn't get her to give up her ties to the Resistance.

Kara nibbled on his lips. *You initiated this. Don't tell me you don't know what we are doing, my mate.*

When I'm with you like this, nothing else matters. When I'm not with you, I long for you. You are the only thing that matters to me. Acknowledging the deepness of his feelings for her only made him feel them all the more strongly.

He watched as she closed her eyes and buried her head in his shoulder. She let out a soft shuddering breath.

A sharp pain momentarily went through his heart and just as quickly, it disappeared. He felt a calming soothing healing balm of love cover him just as he was starting to doubt that Kara felt the same way about him.

For a minute he'd been frightened he didn't matter as much to his mate. Then just like that, he felt her love for him, tentative though it was. His mate had come to care for him just as much as he cared for her.

She opened her eyes and pools of emotion and desire fell out. *I love you, Darwu. Please tell me you know I speak the truth.*

I do. Dawru thrust his hips lifting her and pinning her to the door with each upward motion. *I know you love me. You can't help it. You're mine, Kara, all mine.*

All yours. Yes. "Ye—es!" Kara let out the word in a scream as her sex tightened around him and an orgasm rippled through her. She let out a soft moan and wrapped her arms around him.

The timbre of her voice, the viselike grip of her sex, and the love pouring from her heart, all worked together to send Darwu over the edge. He'd wanted so very much to prolong the encounter, but he found himself thrusting at a rapid pace and losing any semblance of control as the semen gushed from him in large spurts.

He held on to Kara afterward, afraid to let go, afraid it was all a dream and he hadn't really found his mate. Only a few days ago he'd been miserable and alone. And now he knew happiness unlike anything he had ever known; and he owed it all to the little rebel in his arms. As he caressed Kara's soft lean body, Darwu peered into her head looking for anything that would show him his happiness wasn't going to last long.

Kara slid down from her little nook between the door and Darwu muscular frame unable to believe she had actually made love against a door.

As her feet finally touched the ground, she felt him, probing, pushing up against her barriers, snooping around in her head. Kara retreated to the secret space in her mind as she smiled at Darwu and walked away.

Every time she found herself letting down her guard and becoming happy with Darwu, he reminded her he was still the Warrior Prince, still a royal, and all of her love wouldn't change any of that.

Reminded that The Resistance and the people of Ourlane needed her to be alert and to fight until the end, she kept her head up and kept moving.

Where are you going? Darwu spoke the words in her head in a soft whisper.

"To bed." Kara refused to communicate with the trickster prince in her mind. No way would she let him lull her into a false sense of security while he tried to pick her brains. Hadn't he taken enough already? It hurt even more that he had used the period after their love making, when she'd felt so close to him to probe her mind.

Let's save the bed for last. I have one more thing I want to show you. Right behind her now, Darwu's arms circled her and pulled her tightly against him.

Kara could feel his hard erection in her back, and she wondered what else could he possibly have to show her?

They moved together towards the dresser with a large mirror above it. Darwu moved the oils, scents, and figurines from the dresser with one swipe of his arm as he leaned Kara forward so that only her torso now draped the dresser. Instinctively, her head tilted up and she watched him behind her through the mirror.

Yes, that's right, my mate, now I can see your pretty face while I take you from behind. He entered her then in one powerful thrust.

Kara's eyes widened as she watched Darwu working in and out, over and over, harder and faster. She arched and pushed back to meet his thrusts, relishing the contact so much she soon was standing on her tip toes so that he could reach deeper inside of her.

And all the while he kept his eyes on her through the mirror. Enthralled, she couldn't look away until she felt him again, full assault digging into her mind.

Closing her eyes momentarily, Kara opened them and met him full gaze. She wrapped herself around his probe, studying his warrior-like prowl in her head as she moved her hips back to take more of him in her body.

Following his signal back into his own head, Kara was surprised to see all the love there. How could he possibly love her when he was using her most vulnerable time to probe her mind?

She knew he was only searching because he wanted her to stay alive and the king had threatened to kill her if she couldn't be trusted. But he was her mate. He was supposed to talk to her about this kind of thing, not ambush her brain when she least expected it. Right?

She supposed she was getting stronger because she was able to go deeper into his head all the while keeping her gaze on him through the mirror and meeting his powerful thrusts as he took her against the dresser.

Poking around in his head when he had no idea she was doing it, or that she could, made her feel a little guilty, but then she figured he was doing almost the same thing, nosing around without permission.

Kara followed the patterns of his brain with fascination. Her mate was a warrior through and through. He was always plotting and planning. As he probed her head, he did so in order to save her life. He wasn't going to let anyone take Kara away from him, not even Kara herself.

His determination almost made her retreat, leave his head, and confess her newfound abilities. Until she remembered the people of Ourlane needed her. She was their last hope. She needed to gather as much information as she could from her mate and hope the Divine would forgive her for taking advantage of their sacred union in such a manner.

"Ah," Kara let out the sound against her will as Darwu stroked the same hot spot in her repeatedly with his deep powerful plunges. He reached his hand around her body and gently rubbed her clitoris as he continued to hit the same spot over and over.

Losing all thoughts of probing his mind, Kara got lost in the building feelings Darwu's lovemaking brought out. "OH! DAR-WU!" The last moan was trapped in her throat as Darwu sent one more thrust into her and the warm gush of his seed exploded inside of her. Kara felt herself tightening around him as her orgasm ripped through her body.

Laying her head on the dresser, she figured she could just sleep there for a moment because she was truly spent. She wouldn't be able to move for quite some time.

Then she felt Darwu wrapping her in his arms and carrying her to the bed. He held her until he fell asleep. Kara couldn't help but wonder if they really had a chance at happiness as she used his rested state to go exploring in his head.

"It's her. She is the one. She must be cloaking herself somehow, but I have picked up spurts and bursts of her power briefly. Already she is changing the dynamic of the castle and she is not even utilizing her full power yet." Prince Alto's grave expression and somber tone did not please the king at all.

The king surveyed the candles on the altar in the secret Cultide ceremony room behind the hidden door in his chambers. The six ever-burning candles which were supposed to protect the castle and keep the rule of the Cultide strong had decreased from six to three with two having fallen over. A slight crack made its way across the strong wooden altar. Even when they tried to re-light the candles they wouldn't burn. The girl's power already struggled with the Cultide for dominance and she hadn't even fully shown herself.

The king had to make a difficult decision, and he didn't want to make it. If he did, his son would lose his sacred mate, again. The king could also lose his own mate. Surely the queen would never speak to him again if she didn't get a grandchild before they rid themselves of the girl.

You promised me, Milo. And what is the big deal? Can't you just put her through the Cultide ceremony like you did with me? She's a shamaness not the Divine itself for goodness sake!

I thought you were sleeping? Go back to sleep, Hietha. This doesn't concern you.

Yes it does. Even if the girl has the power you all seem to think she has, you can get her to our side. First you need to get Darwu. Bring him into the Cultide and he can bring his mate.

Everything has to happen in its time, Hietha. Darwu will be the strongest leader of our line. The power in him is great. The Cultide will corrupt it and make it even greater. A ruler such as that would not wait idly for his father to die. Bringing our son into the fold now would be the equivalent of signing my death certificate.

And you think killing his mate wouldn't do the same thing? Yes, my son is powerful. But he is still my son, our son. We need to—

Enough, Hietha. I have council for this. You need to leave me and—

Council? You call that idiot, power-hungry brother of yours council? Fine, have it your way. But if you kill the girl before she's served her purpose, you'll see that she wasn't the only shamaness you had to worry about after all. Just because I allowed you to corrupt my powers does not mean that I will let you rob me of this one joy.

She was gone, closing her mind to him in the most abrupt and halting way she could.

Sighing, the king rubbed his hand across his forehead.

Bewildered, Prince Alto quipped, "Hietha?"

"Yes, be happy brother that you weren't born first and therefore skipped the fate of having a shrew of a shamaness for a wife." The king knew his mate would be angry with him. But she was a woman after all and she had no idea what was really at stake. The entire way they had ruled for centuries could change and he couldn't allow it.

"I suppose there has to be some drawback in being the ruler of the land. But your Hietha and this Kara girl are two very different sorts of shamanesses." Prince Alto stood and stretched. "For the most part, their powers can be corrupted as to not cause trouble in the Cultide's reign. This has been the case for generations. But every once and a while one shows up who can't be corrupted. We have been able to foresee these and have gotten rid of them in the past. But this one . . . Just from the glimpses I'm getting of her power, she is a strong one."

Suddenly tired of thinking about the entire thing and sure the problem of handling the girl would be easily decided, the king stood, dismissing his comments. "Shamanesses bleed red just like everyone else. We'll watch her for now and if the power begins to shift too much, we will have no choice but to kill her the same way we killed her parents, and the same way we will gut her worthless rebel uncle."

When Kara opened her eyes the next morning, she found Darwu had already left. Briefly thanking the Divine she would be able to search for her uncle and the others without having to explain anything or make up any excuses, she hurried to bathe and dress before her mate came back.

Just as she was putting on her leather pants and tunic, a knock sounded at the door to their suite. Swearing to herself, she walked over to the door.

"Yes," she mumbled softly as she opened the door.

"Princess Kara, it's me, Donia. I have the first of your new clothes made and ready for you to wear. While I'm sure you looked lovely in the dress last night, I have the feeling you don't want to wear it again."

Kara couldn't help smiling. She'd told Donia not to worry about staying up all night to make her something 'suitable' to wear, but the seamstress had done so anyway. Stepping aside, she let Donia in also keeping in mind that she needed to get rid of the woman because she had resisters to set free.

"Donia, you really shouldn't have stayed up all night to make this dress. I . . ." Kara's jaw dropped when she saw the garment Donia had in her hands. If beauty could be mixed with durability, mobility, and warrior-flair, Donia had done so in the outfit she designed. Not really a dress and not really the leather pants and tunic she was used to, the outfit incorporated the best elements of both.

Donia smiled. "I'll take that as a sign you like what you see, Princess."

Reaching out to touch the beautiful garment, Kara barely contained her gasp. "It's wonderful. I had no idea that such a thing could be made."

"Please try it on, Princess, I am dying to see how it looks on you." Handing Kara the gown and clasping her hands together in excitement, Donia stepped further into the room.

"Fine I will, but please call me Kara. And we'll need to hurry because I have something I need to do." Kara felt bad rushing Donia, but she had to rescue her uncle and his men.

Donia's eyes narrowed slightly and Kara worried she'd said too much. She didn't know the seamstress, but felt she could trust the woman with her life. Besides Darwu, Donia was the only person in the castle who gave off positive vibes.

"Are you going to try and see your—your friends being held captive?"

"Yes." Hesitating briefly, Kara decided to trust the woman. "Please don't say anything. I feel that I can trust you. I don't know why. But I feel like I can. If you tell the royals what I'm doing, then they will surely kill me before I can free the others. I can't let that happen. The Resistance needs my uncle alive and fighting."

"The Resistance needs *you*, Kara Millan," Donia said the words with such conviction it became more than evident she believed not only what she said but she believed in the cause. "I won't say anything, but you have to promise me you will be careful and you won't let anything happen to you. Take care and caution and remember if anything happens, you have it in you to make sure the Divine will be done."

Puzzled, Kara shook her head. "I don't know what you mean."

"You *do* know what I mean." Donia placed her hand over Kara's heart and pressed. "Deep in here you know. It's time for you to stop hiding, little one. Now, let's get you dressed so you can see exactly how warrior princess-friendly this garment is. There are hidden pockets and compartments for you to place small weapons, because you never know when you might need them. But once you remember who you are, you won't need weapons."

Kara followed the eager woman. Although she didn't have a clue what Donia meant, something in the conviction of the woman's voice touched her. She got the same urgent feeling she used to get in the bush when fighting for the people, the feeling she should be doing more. She tried to put her finger on what Donia's words brought out of her and couldn't.

Kara felt Donia knew exactly who she was. She was part of The Resistance and she was a warrior. She may be the mate of a royal, but she would never forsake the people of Ourlane.

Darwu refused to let his guard down around his two cousins. They had been at him non-stop with questions about Kara. Did he really believe she was his sacred mate? Why did the rebels allow her to live if their plans were to harm the monarchy by insuring that Darwu went mateless? And why would they send her back now?

Though they posed as though they had nothing but his best interests at heart, Darwu knew without a doubt, that Gab and Jorge would like nothing more than to see his demise.

He'd never allowed his cousins to get to him before. But now— now that he had a mate—everything was different. Darwu turned to Gab, pretended to listen and willed his father to arrive so they could begin the council. Why they needed to have yet another council was beyond him. They had already decided the fate of the prisoners.

"For your sake, cousin, I hope she is who she says she is and you don't end up regretting you didn't have her gutted with the rest of the rebel swine. The king seemed adamant about holding you responsible if she is still aligned with The Resistance." Neither Jorge's voice or expression held any hint that he truly cared about Darwu's fate. The man leaned against the wall staring at his fingernails as if he had found the greatest treasures of Ourlane in his useless hands.

"Well, I for one am against waiting around to see if she does something to turn on us. My mate and my children are in this castle. What if the rebel whore does something to harm them? Who has to die before we slit—"

Darwu didn't give Gab a moment to finish his tirade before his fist landed across Gab's jaw knocking the man out of his seat.

Gab tumbled to the floor and let out a howl as he leaped on to Darwu, clutching and scratching like a woman. Darwu landed methodic blows to Gab's upper torso winding him and causing him to fall back against the table.

Jorge reached between them trying to break them up and Darwu offered him a jab for his troubles. As angry as he was, he knew he could take them both on with no problem. He knocked one down and then the other until his father and uncle entered the room.

"Enough! What is going on here? Have you no sense? You are grown men not little boys!" The king's anger permeated through the room.

Yet, Darwu found he had to hit Gab one last time before stopping. Glancing at his father's harsh stare, Darwu tried to at least appear sorry, if for nothing else than for getting caught giving his cousins the thrashing they deserved.

"This won't do at all. One day you will reign as King of Ourlane and as you have no siblings, your first cousins will act as your council. For the three of you to be fighting in this manner doesn't bode well for the future of Ourlane." Prince Alto tsked and narrowed his eyes accusingly at Darwu.

While he was able to hold back his response that under no circumstance would he ever accept council from Gab and Jorge, Darwu couldn't halt the hiss that escaped his lips.

Gab wiped blood from his mouth bitterly and gave Darwu a hateful glance. "Oh don't worry, Father. He's Darwu the Warrior Prince; he won't need any council from the likes of us. He'd probably accept council from his rebel whore of a mate first!"

Darwu socked Gab in the mouth again and sent him spiraling to the floor.

"Enough! Darwu, leave the council now! Until you know how to contain yourself, do not come back." The king banged his hand on the wooden table hard enough to make the glasses on the table fall and break.

"But, Father—"

The king shook his head and pointed towards the door. "No, Darwu. I won't have you making a mockery of this council or this throne!"

Narrowing his eyes on his father and knowing he treaded on ground he'd never walked before, Darwu snapped. "Would you allow any man to insult your mate the way that Gab has insulted mine?"

"That is not the point." The clipped pointed tone of voice offered the only hint that the king had had enough of Darwu. "You will have to find better ways to deal with your cousin's taunts. They mean you no harm. Your uncle is right. They are your future council. Now leave us."

Darwu stormed out of the room. If he could have hit Gab again without incurring more of the king's wrath, he would have.

"Well, that didn't go very well." Prince Alto shook his head in disgust.

Taking his seat, the king leaned back. The girl would have to go. "No, it didn't. He is already so far gone with her, I have no doubt she is either his sacred mate or the most powerful spell casting shamaness in the Providence of Ourlane."

"Given the prophecy, brother, his mate and that shamaness are one and the same." Prince Alto's ironic tone and sarcastic smirk made the king want to knock him down the way Darwu had just beaten the two idiots Alto called sons.

"We could force her through the Cultide ceremony and try to corrupt her power. So far she is showing so very little of it. If it weren't for the subtle changes and shifts I can already feel in the castle, one would never know she was the prophesied one." Jorge sat at the council table not bothering to wipe away the blood dripping from his nose.

Gab limped towards the table and bitterly sniped, "Or we could just slit her pathetic little throat and Darwu's too if he wants to put all of our futures at risk because of a silly piece of ass."

The king glared at his idiot nephew. Killing Darwu and naming one of these fools his heir was not an option. Darwu would have to pick from one of their progeny for his successor. At least Darwu would have the chance to groom and choose carefully. Hopefully Gab and Jorge's sons wouldn't be half the screw-ups their fathers were.

"You know, I find myself wondering on a daily basis, if you really could possibly be as stupid as you appear. Why would you provoke Darwu in that manner? Why would you, who have a mate, and know the depths of that kind of connection, call another man's mate a whore and be surprised when he beats the crap out of you." The king didn't expect his nephew to answer the questions. He just needed to ask them.

"Taking her through the ceremony is an option. If we can't corrupt her then, we can easily kill her while we have her there. We'd have to find something to do with Darwu though. If he had any inkling of what we are thinking, who knows what he might do." Prince Alto offered hesitantly.

"I'm sure we can find a way to keep Darwu busy." *Can't we Hietha?* The king knew his nosey wife was lurking as usual.

Milo, I'm so glad you have finally seen things my way and decided to take the girl through the Cultide corrupting ceremony. But I can't talk with you now. My darling son is visiting with me. You really shouldn't have yelled at him for striking those imbecile nephews of yours. And she was gone.

"So, we'll plan to take her through the ceremony as soon as possible. I'm thinking tomorrow would be good. If it works, we can have her present for the slaughter of her uncle and the others, it would bode well for the message we want to send." The king tried to have some hope in a situation that seemed to be getting bleaker and bleaker.

"Yes, I just hope that works." Prince Alto nodded in agreement.

"Me to," the king said more to himself than to his brother or nephews.

Chapter 13

Walking carefully down the dark corridors in the castle's dungeon, Kara moved with a warrior's stealth. She'd dodged several of the king's men and was close to the cell where her uncle and the others were being held.

"Are you supposed to be down here, Princess?"

Kara jumped at the sound of a male voice behind her. It was one of the soldiers who had caught her snooping around Darwu's camp just a few days ago and brought her to Darwu. Did the man have some kind of honing device on her or something? How did he manage to catch her when she didn't want to be caught?

Keeping her appearance calm and disinterested, Kara lied, "My mate has given me permission to have one last talk with my uncle before his execution."

"The prince has not left word with me, Princess. I'm afraid I can't let you see any of the rebels unless I hear it directly from the prince. So if you would kindly find your way back upstairs the way you found your way down." The soldier walked around her and stood directly in front of her blocking her way in the narrow hallway.

"I'm going to see my uncle. So unless you want to physically stop me." Kara paused and gave him a pointed stare of warning. "And mind you, the Warrior Prince wouldn't take it well if you did. Not to mention the fact I intend to fight you if you put a hand on me."

"Let me see . . . risk a tussle with you or have the king take my head for letting your see the rebels. Hmm, I think I'll take what ever you have to offer, *Princess*." The way the soldier snidely spat out the word "princess" showed he wasn't the least bit concerned about Kara doing him any damage.

Excellent, Kara thought. An unsuspecting mark was the best kind. Taking a step around him, Kara continued on her way to the cell holding her uncle and the others.

She'd come too close to turn back. At first she only wanted to see them, to assure them she hadn't willingly betrayed them and see if they had a plan to break free.

Only one guard was on duty, and a cocky one at that, giving her a new sense of hope. She would take care of him and then set her uncle and the others free. The day was looking brighter and brighter. She even started to hum softly as she walked.

The soldier grabbed her shoulder. She gave a backward kick, catching him in the groin. The soldier let out a yelp and Kara spun before rising and kicking him in the face.

His head jolted back. He righted himself quickly, wiping blood from his nose, glaring at Kara. Taking several steps back, she knelt into a battle pose. Settled and ready to pounce as soon as the soldier made his next move, Kara jumped and took off in a spurt when he lunged at her.

Just missing his strike, she circled him. As she came around to the front of him, he reached out and grabbed her hair. Kara bent her head down, leaning into his pull. Lulling him into thinking she wouldn't resist, she raised her arm, catching him off guard. The swift chopping motion of her arm caused a soft, subtle snap in his. He muttered a curse as he let go of her hair and grabbed his broken arm with his other hand.

Taking fair use of every advantage, she kicked him again in the groin and the face. He fell on the concrete floor head-first, knocking him out.

Smiling and relishing the thrill of the fight that she had been missing, Kara grabbed the keys from his waist and ran over to the cell.

"Uncle! I've come to free you."

Startled, her uncle stared at her in momentary shock before an expression of anger laced his face. "What are you doing here, Kara? Why did you risk everything in this foolish attempt to save us from our destinies?"

Taken aback, Kara paused. "What? They plan to kill you all in a matter of days. I can't sit by and let that happen. I won't. The Resistance needs you. The people need you!"

For the first time she could ever remember, her uncle glared at Her and didn't seem to listen to her. "The people need you, Kara! They need you to stop hiding and come into yourself! If you don't, then there is no hope for the people and we will have died for nothing."

"You are not going to die, Uncle. I am getting you out of here." Kara didn't understand. Rafe was the leader of The Resistance. The people needed him far more than they needed her.

"You are betraying the trust of your sacred mate and denying your destiny by attempting this. Leave now before you make matters worse." Rafe waved his hand in a dismissive manner and turned his back to her.

Confused, Kara resorted to begging. "I don't understand, Uncle, please let me help you. Is it because you think I betrayed you? I didn't! He got into my head and I couldn't stop him then. But I have figured out a way to shield my thoughts now. I can get you out of here and—"

Rafe turned around glowering as he snapped, "Shielding, hiding, cloaking, that is what you have been doing for years, Kara! The time has come for you to stop hiding. If you are not ready to do that, then you can't help anyone, not even yourself. You need to be working with your mate to uncover your full self, not hiding from him. Let the prince help you to remember who you are, Princess."

"Stop calling me that! Uncle, please . . ." Kara moved to unlock the cell with tears streaming down her face.

"No!" Rafe walked toward the back of the cell, turning his back on her again. "Leave here now, Kara. Do as I told you and don't come back. I have my destiny to fulfill and you have yours. Stop hiding from it. Get your mate to help you."

Turning, Kara dropped the keys and started to run away from the cell. A multitude of feelings bombarded her at once. She knew she'd failed The Resistance, but she hadn't thought her uncle would turn his back on her.

Vision blurred and distraught, she didn't even realize she wasn't alone in the hallway until, someone grabbed her.

"Look what we have here, Jorge. I know the new princess has a good reason for being in the dungeon when no one gave her permission to be down here." Gab wrapped his arms around her and she felt a tide of disgust overcome her.

Shaking herself away from Gab, she was automatically grabbed by the somewhat stronger Jorge.

"If I were the two of you, I would keep my hands to myself." Giving Gab a menacing glare, she tried to wrestle herself away from Jorge who was holding on like a vise. "You already look like someone has pummeled you. Don't make me add to it."

"Oh, it seems like our little princess needs some training in the manners department, brother. That mouth of hers needs taming. What kind of cousins would we be not to help Dawru out a bit with that." Gab hauled off and slapped her across the face.

"Gab!" Jorge shouted giving Kara the distraction she needed to lift her foot and kick back into his shin.

He loosened his hold of her a bit and she turned kicking him in the groin as she brought her fist upwards, pressing his nose clear into his eyes.

Jorge fell back cursing and Gab took that opportunity to come at her again.

"This slut needs to learn a lesson," Gab said as he pulled his fist back aiming to punch Kara.

Kara grabbed the arm as it moved forward and used her grip to flip him.

Don't bore me with drivel. Fight, swine! Kara thought as she readied herself for their next assault. She was going to be in a lot of trouble anyway, so she might just as well kick their asses while she was at it.

Kara, what are you doing?

Kara cursed as she realized being in battle mode made her forget to block the mind-wandering mate from her thoughts.

Both Jorge and Gab were up and coming at her. She backed away, readied herself for assault, and tried to placate her mate at the same time. *I can't talk right now. I'm kind of busy.*

Busy doing what? Darwu's words had an angry edge.

Gab sucker-punched her in the stomach and Kara bent in pain as Jorge grabbed her hair and pulled her backwards.

"Don't hit her again, Gab. Let's just take her to Father and Uncle. We need to start the corrupting—"

"I think we should just kill her now and be done with it." Gab punched her in the stomach again.

Kara blocked out the searing pain in her gut as best she could and summoned strength from the pit of her soul. Luckily, Darwu had taken the hint and stopped asking questions because she had no time to answer.

Kara shook herself vigorously out of Jorge's grasp.

Jorge backed away, looking behind her. "Listen, Princess, we were just trying to help you. You had no business down here, especially without your mate's permission."

"I don't need anyone's permission! I can go anywhere I please. And right now, I'm about to *going* to pummel the both of you!" Kara readied herself to lunge forward and was halted mid-stride by a pair of strong hands she knew automatically didn't belong to that weakling Gab.

So you don't need anyone's permission? Odd, I seem to think you need at least one person's permission to go traipsing off into the dungeon. And I don't recall my mate asking for my permission.

Darwu firmly held her in his grasp and spoke his menacing words in her head.

Not able to think of any believable excuse, Kara just considered herself caught.

Anger didn't even begin to describe the mix of emotions swirling through Darwu's mind as he held his conniving and traitorous mate.

When he'd gotten an inkling of where she was and the danger she'd been in, he gone rushing out of his mother's quarters in search of her.

She apparently had some sort of block up and he couldn't get much of a read on her.

Glancing at his cousins, he could tell Kara had done a decent job at continuing the thrashing he'd given them earlier that day and he felt a moment of pride in her.

Spinning Kara around so to face him, Darwu wished he had trusted his instincts about   . The key was finding out why and how she managed to do so.

When he glimpsed her face he felt steam coming from his ears. Her lip was spilt. His face became so knotted in rage he couldn't contain it. The rage bubbled over when he realized someone had struck her in the face. Letting Kara go he grabbed Gab and jacked him up against the wall. Reason told him only Gab would be stupid enough to strike Kara.

"Now, cousin, before you wallop me, I think you should consider that your mate was down here where she clearly had no business. And she is a part of the rebel resistance. Any other—" Gab started blabbering on and Darwu interrupted him with a punch to the jaw.

"She is not any other person. She is my mate. Mine to punish. You should have left her alone and come to me. Or did you not hear me when I told my father, *the king*, that I would have sovereignty over my mate!" Darwu punched him again. "Do you think you rank above the king?" The next connection between Darwu's fist and Gab's face caused Gab to pass out.

Dawru let the weakling slip to the floor and turned to face Jorge.

"I didn't strike your mate." Jorge whimpered in a pleading tone as he backed away.

"Liar, when I came in you had your hands on her," Darwu said as he took steps toward Jorge.

"Yes, I held her to keep her from hitting me. Look at my face, Cousin. That—that—mate of yours fights like no other princess I've ever seen. What was I supposed to do, let her keep whaling on me? I did the best I could without striking her myself. And I apologize for my brother." Jorge took giant steps backwards before turning and taking off in a mad dash.

Darwu debated whether he should chase his cousin or not. Soon, the king would find out about Kara being down in the dungeon meaning Darwu only had a short period of time to find out exactly what she had been doing and to punish her sufficiently for her betrayal. He could not afford to have her betray him again.

Turning to Kara and noticing for the first time how sexy she looked in one of Donia newly created leather and mud cloth get-ups, he had the perfect idea for getting the truth out of Kara once and for all.

A hesitant smiled crossed her lips as she took tentative steps towards him. "I'm so glad you found me. I got lost in this huge place and I was scared," she said as she buried herself in his arms. "And then your cousins found me and I thought they were going to help. But they didn't. Oh, Darwu, I'm so glad you saved me from those horrid men."

147

Darwu didn't need to probe her mind to know she was lying through her teeth. Clasping her shoulders, he pushed her back slightly to get a good look at her face. She appeared neither frightened nor grateful to have been found.

Darwu took her by the hand and led her through the hallway. Stopping for a moment he looked down at his cousin, Gab, still knocked out on the floor. He let go of Kara's hand and lifted Gab from the floor. "Follow me."

Glad that his mate had the common sense to do as she was told this time, Darwu carried his cousin back to the cells and placed him in an empty one after finding the keys on the ground in front of the rebel cell. Darwu glanced at his groaning soldier and shot Kara as menacing a look as he could muster before picking up the soldier and placing him in the cell with Gab. After locking the cell door, he walked over to Kara.

You have been a very bad little mate. Darwu spoke the words to her mind as he mentally caressed her soul. *You do realize you will have to be punished?*

"Darwu—"

And you should know I am keeping count of all of your infractions, mate. You will only make it worse if you continue to lie.

Her eyes widened slightly and she nibbled her lower lip. He could feel the contemplation in her head. The thoughts circled around in her brain at a furious pace before she tilted her head and let out a sigh. She didn't say anything and Darwu was almost disappointed.

He took her hand and led her further back into the corridors of the dungeon. Brokering no argument, she followed.

Once they reached the room he was looking for, Darwu exhaled. He could not turn back now. His mate needed serious training in obedience and control and he was just the man to tame her.

Chapter 14

Kara gasped in spite of all her attempts at bravery once they stepped into the room. From what she could tell based on the shadows forming in the darkness, it was some kind of torture chamber. Once Darwu lit some candles in the room, she let out a sharp hiss of air. It was a torture chamber, *a sexual torture chamber.*

Eyes wide and mouth open, she tried to think of a way to appease her mate so he would forget what she now clearly read in his mind. He intended to wear her down both physically and mentally. He wanted her tamed and obedient.

Backing away towards the door, Kara smiled as pleasantly as she could muster, especially since she could tell what he was thinking and what he had planned for her. She tried to figure out a way to change his mind without letting on that she actually knew what he was thinking.

"This is an interesting room," she offered as she backed into the door and touched the doorknob.

Darwu took two giant steps blocking her. He took her hand and removed it from the door. "Going somewhere, mate?"

Letting her eyes roam the room and taking in all the weirdly shaped pieces of furniture with straps and buckles, along with the paddles, whips, chains, ropes, and phallic shapes displayed throughout the room, Kara closed her eyes and paused before answering. "No, but I figured we should go back upstairs. I mean, we wouldn't want anyone to worry about us."

The dangerous glint in his eyes along with his thoughts, all centered around which piece of furniture he was going to strap her onto first, made Kara's heart race.

Glancing around the room again, her eyes landed on a large table covered in black rubber and lots of straps. She peered at it and quickly turned her head. Unfortunately, Darwu noticed her gaze and at that moment he made his decision on which piece of furniture to use first.

Leading her by the hand to the huge table in the center of the room, he placed a firm kiss on her lips. *I'm going to need you to take off Donia's splendid creation first and then we're going to have a few lessons.*

Les-les—sons. Kara had no idea thoughts could stutter. But the thought of being tied to that table while Darwu tried out the devilish things that were running through his mind caused her thoughts to bounce across her head.

Kissing her again, his hands worked the buttons on her clothing until the entire new frock lay at her feet and she stood before him naked. *Yes. You're going to learn how to control yourself and by doing so, you're going to learn to obey me.*

"Dawru—"

Unh, unh, unh. Remember, we don't want to make this harder than it needs to be. Although they say the hardest lessons learned are the least forgotten. I'm sure you can tell I'm very upset with you right now. And I know you don't want to make me any more upset. Or maybe you do? Dawru lifted her to the table and started strapping her onto it.

Kara closed her eyes, awaiting her torture. And torture it was going to be because her mate intended to tease her with his hands and mouth until she was ready to come and then stop, over and over again until she was delirious with need for release. He intended to deny her repeatedly after bringing her to the brink of pleasure. He intended to do this until she broke and let him into every part of her mind and until she agreed to keep no more secrets from him.

Knowing what he intended, Kara could only hope she was strong enough to take it. None of her warrior training prepared her for this kind of torture.

His strong hands began to trail her body, slowly, caressing her. Stopping at her stomach, Darwu face took on an angry glare. The thoughts of rage and murder crossing his mind in a red haze almost made her afraid.

"You're badly bruised here. What happened? Did Gab hit you here?" Although the words were bitten out between clenched teeth, he applied a soft gentle touch to the bruises.

Not knowing what to say, in response she settled for the truth. "Yes, but he was only able to get in the punches because the other idiot held me."

Murder. Rage. Anger. All of these combined in Darwu mind as he turned and walked toward the door.

Kara knew he was going to go kill his cousin and while she would have gladly liked to kill the fool herself, she knew there would be no turning back from such an act. Maybe the king would kill her and the rest of The Resistance and maybe he had threatened Darwu, but if there was a chance that the king would show mercy on his son, she knew it wouldn't happen if Darwu killed the two lesser princes.

Clearing her throat, she sighed. "Darwu, please don't leave me here alone, especially not tied to this table and unable to defend myself. What if your cousin Jorge comes back to finish what he started? You know he has probably rescued Gab from the cell already. I don't want to be strapped to this table naked when those two return."

Darwu calmed slightly and his mind slowly returned to her and the taming task he plotted.

Kara let out a hiss. What on earth possessed her to sacrifice herself for the evil tax collectors?

Darwu came back to the table, glanced at her stomach and took a deep breath. "I am going to kill Gab for harming you. But first, we need to make sure you learn your lesson as well. You had no business coming down to the dungeon and trying to free the rebels. You need to learn self-control and discipline."

"I have plenty of self-control and discipline. I simply wanted to say good—"

Darwu's mouth clamped over her left breast, sucking the nipple into his mouth as his hand slid down her stomach into the slick folds of her womanhood.

His fingers cradled her sex and rocked deep inside of her. The rhythm of his penetrating hands and silky mouth made her lift her hips off the table so that his fingers could delve deeper.

In a matter of minutes she felt her sex begin to tighten against his fingers and she arched to ready herself for the full impact of the orgasm she knew was coming. Just as she neared the breaking point, Darwu removed his hand and her breast fell out of his mouth with a pop.

Even though she'd had some idea about what her mate had planned for her, going through it was more torturous than she ever could have imagined. She sighed as she felt the slowly built energy inside her dissipate back into nothingness, leaving behind only the yearning for completion she now realized her mate wouldn't grant until she broke down and gave him full access to her mind, heart, and soul.

Control is a funny thing, mate. You see, sometimes it's best to relinquish it to someone else, someone more capable of seeing to your needs. And sometimes, if you learn to control yourself, you will learn when it's best to give up that control.

You're talking in foolish riddles, Darwu, and making no sense at all. Why don't you just give up and lock me away with the others and be done with it? Surely it would be better than this nonsense. I'm never going to allow you to control me. Never. Kara jerked at the straps holding her firmly and tried to kick out with her legs.

It's okay, mate. We have all evening. We'll see if you come to see things a bit differently in the morning. And the pun is very much intended. Darwu's words licked her mind as his mouth clamped her sex and his tongue began a sensuous dance with her clit.

Each lick, each flick caused heat to build. His stiff tongue buried itself inside of her as his hands toyed with her. Together the movements of his mouth and hands brought her to the peak, and she felt as if she might burst into a million pieces. At the moment he pulled his lips and fingers away.

Kara let out a scream of incompletion. Soft shuddering breaths escaped her lips and she turned her head to the side, refusing to look her torturer in the eye.

Once you learn you are meant to do my will, you will be able to control your urges to assert your own will. Control would have stopped you from coming down to the dungeon. Control would have stopped you from trying to free your uncle and the rest of the rebels. And a little self control would have you experiencing your second orgasm right now instead of almost being brought to the brink a third time only to be denied. Darwu brought his mouth down over her sex again, this time climbing up onto the table and reaching up to cup her breasts with both his hands while he suckled.

Again he waited until she was almost ready to explode before he pulled away.

He repeated his torture and all she could do was take it, hoping against hope he would pull away too late and she would be able to find release at least once. The torture must have gone on for hours, until she was delirious with want and need. She needed to experience an orgasm so bad she realized she would have done anything and promised anything just to have Darwu straddle her and bring her to completion.

Dawru walked away from the table and came back with one of the phallic pieces. Gazing at it with glazed over eyes, Kara knew the thing wouldn't come close to satisfying her the way Darwu could. But if he pulled it out too late then maybe, just maybe she would find a small measure of release.

Darwu inserted the dildo slowly into her sex, penetrating her deeply and pulling it out. Working up a steady pace, he worked her to the point where she'd begun to clench desperately around the torture toy.

A soft moan came through her lips, just as Darwu removed the dildo.

She'd come so close to reaching her peak, so close she almost wanted to cry when he took it away. Then he started again, moving the phallus in and out, over and over, stopping as soon as her body started to shake with desire. After the fifth time, Kara screamed. "Please, Dawru. Stop this."

Do you want to come, mate? Darwu softly murmured in her mind.

Yes. Yes. Please. Yes.

Then you need to open everything up to me now. Show me all you have been hiding the past two days. I know you have a spot of yourself closed to me and I want to see it all.

Kara closed her eyes tightly. She couldn't show him everything. Then she would have nothing left. No place left to hide. No freedom from his constant presence in her head. No she couldn't let him into her safe spot.

Seeing her refusal to cooperate, Darwu threw the dildo to the floor and thrust two fingers deeply inside her, rubbing her clit with his thumb. He worked her diligently, bringing his mouth down to lick the sweat of frustration off her skin. The touch of his tongue was too much for her. She felt herself nearing an explosion so intense she had to grit her teeth not to yell. And no sooner than she felt the release of her sexual tension, Darwu removed his hand and halted his licking.

A tear trailed down her face in spite of all the warrior strength and fortitude she thought she possessed. Darwu had won; she couldn't take it anymore. Slowly she let her barriers fall and gave him full access to everything in her secret space.

She watched the growing anger transform his face. His eyes narrowed and his teeth formed a snarl. She felt him stomping angrily around her mind and knew when he discovered that she could block him out at will now.

Her head felt as though it would explode when he found out that she not only could get into his head but also had been there and was still there.

So you are a little witch, aren't you? You have figured out a way into your mate's head without even giving birth. Darwu thought in his own head knowing she could hear him. He released the straps that held her to the table.

And you were going to free your uncle and the others. You have betrayed me, mate, and you will be punished. He lifted her from the table, slung her over his shoulder walked over to the wall that held the whips and paddles. *Clearly my hand didn't do a good job in making you see the error of your ways. Let's see what shall we use to finish off your lesson for today.*

Kara wiggled and started to kick. She'd sworn she wouldn't take anymore spankings from Darwu and she fully intended to keep her word. His hand landed sharply on her bare backside.

Keep still, Kara. I'm trying to pick out the most suitable tool. Since I don't want to hurt you, only see that you learn your lesson, we'll go with this small round paddle. It will hurt only slightly more than the flat of my hand. And hopefully it will be enough to get you to stop behaving foolishly. Darwu sat down on the bench and quickly flipped her from his shoulder to his lap.

Lying across his lap, she barely had a moment to process anything before the paddle crashed down on the soft round flesh of her behind.

She let out a scream in spite of herself and started to kick and wiggle for freedom. Finding no reprieve from Darwu's strong grasp, she sobbed while the wooden paddle connected with her backside.

He said nothing and thought nothing. His mind was firmly focused on the task of spanking her. Each blow made her jump, bounce and shiver. Her clit and her nipples rubbed against his hard lap and soon she found herself approaching an orgasm.

Thwack. She squirmed and tried to lessen the impact of wood thrashing against her skin, but all she managed to do was excite herself sexually. The irony of her finding her much needed release while Darwu gave her a spanking she'd sworn she'd never get again, was not lost on her. Just when she knew that the next smack of the paddle would make her burst, Darwu stopped.

You are not to come yet. Control, Kara. You will learn about control once and for all. Darwu smoothed his hand over her heated bottom as he spoke the words into her mind.

"I hate you!" Kara screamed to the top of her lungs and found that, to her horror, she was sobbing.

Hate me all you want, mate. But you will respect my wishes and do as you are told or you will know my wrath. You are lucky I care for you as I do, or you would feel the lash kissing your sweet lying, conniving little hide. Dawru stopped the caress of her sore behind and proceeded to spank her with the paddle again.

Thwack. Thwack was the only sound she heard as she tried in vain to move away from the punishing wood. Soon she felt that familiar feeling of impending sexual release and let out a sigh when Darwu stopped.

Darwu stood her up in front of him and then stood himself.

Dejected did not begin to describe her feelings as he walked her over to a tall bench with straps and leaned her over it. He strapped her arms to the front legs of the tall thin bench and after using his own leg to spread her wide, he strapped her legs to the back end of the bench. Bending forward, she couldn't see what Darwu was doing behind her, but she heard him taking off his clothing.

"I want to make love to you now, mate. Do you want me to make love to you?"

Kara couldn't believe how much she wanted him inside of her. She knew that as soon as he penetrated her with his massive penis, she was going to explode into an orgasm.

No, mate. You won't explode into an orgasm. If you want me to make love to you, then you will need to exhibit control. You must control yourself and not come until I tell you to. If you don't think you're going to be able to do that, then I won't be making love to you.

She wanted to yell and scream at him, *fine don't make love to me then*. But she couldn't. She needed to find release and at least if she did things his way, she would eventually find it.

"Good you're learning. Now, if your want me to take you, then ask me to. Tell me what you want, mate." The hard-edged slant in his eyes, the angry curl of his lips, and the harsh tilt of his head all signaled that her mate shouldn't be trifled with at this moment.

And Kara couldn't gather up the strength to resist, deny, or otherwise play that she didn't need him to do exactly what he wanted to her. She wanted it, too. "I want you. Please make love to me, my mate."

Darwu swiftly entered her to the hilt and it was all she could do not to explode with the intrusion.

She gritted her teeth and closed her eyes tightly as Darwu began to piston his hips back and forth.

"I could find my own release and still deny you yours. It would serve you right based on the level of your deceit." The angry words came out of Darwu's mouth in harsh stilted pieces.

He moved his penis in and out of her with such a flurry of thrusts she had to bite down on the inside of her cheek not to come. She stopped when she tasted blood only to bite down again when he hit the spot in her that was always sure to incite an orgasm. What if he did deny her? The delirious state of her head at that moment had her thinking she would surely die if she didn't experience an orgasm soon.

Leaning forward, he whispered in her ear, "You won't die. But perhaps you'll learn a much needed lesson."

He kept hitting the same spot over and over, again and again and soon he reached his hands around her body. One hand found her nipple and the other her clit. The combination had her panting, and for the second time that evening, a tear fell from her eye.

Surrender? Submission? The two words a warrior hated most became her only option.

Darwu, please. I know you're angry, and you have every right to be. I'm sorry. Please forgive me, mate. I can't take anymore of your punishment. I've learned my lesson. She spoke her words in his mind and prayed he would have mercy on her and ease up his thrusts.

Her words only made him take her harder and deeper as he rubbed her clit and pulled her nipple to a point. *I'm going to come now and I want you to come with me, at the same time, not before or after. Now!*

Kara felt her sex tighten and squeeze around him, milking every ounce of his sperm. She shook as the orgasm rocked her from her mind to her toes. And in every place, every space Darwu was present as though they had merged momentarily and became one, connected by their overwhelming orgasms.

The spasms jolting her body under the weight of his still thrusting hips, gave off a rippling effect. She felt surrounded by pools of pleasure all doubled by the energy and fervor radiating from Darwu.

She didn't think the orgasm would ever stop and then she felt it. As their souls, minds and hearts stayed merged together, the waiting egg deep inside of her enveloped his sperm and exploded into two separate identical beings. The breeding of mates had occurred and since she was already in his head, she knew he felt it too. Inside of her, already growing, were twin princes.

Darwu pulled out reluctantly and released the straps. He helped her to stand and turned her to face him. The serious expression on his face made her wonder if he had yet another punishment in store for her.

His hand reached out and touched her belly. "I saw in your mind that your uncle told you that you have some sort of destiny to fulfill. That you have things you need to remember. You have some sort of power he thinks I can help you uncover?"

Kara closed her eyes. She didn't know what her uncle was talking about, but she reasoned that if she was indeed hiding from some part of herself then maybe that was a good thing. She had no intentions of uncovering what she clearly had the good sense to hide.

"No, Kara. We are going to try and find out what you are hiding from yourself. I've been deep in the recesses of your mind and soul,. There was a spot deep inside I couldn't penetrate." Determination filled his voice as he continued. "I will know all of you and have access to all of you, especially now with our sons in your womb."

Fear unlike anything that she'd ever known covered her. She realized she didn't want to remember. "But, Darwu, I don't think this would be wise, especially not now. I don't know why. But I don't feel like it's safe. I feel like I shouldn't let whatever it is inside of me surface."

"Is this fear, coming from Kara, the Warrior Princess." Darwu caressed her cheek. "The very same woman who defied her mate and tried to rescue the rebels? The same woman who knocked out one of my best soldiers and fought my cousins? The same woman who held out so long while being sweetly tortured she almost made her torturer burst from his own growing need? Tell me this is not fear. My mate deserves the title of Warrior Princess who fears nothing and no one." Darwu planted soft sweet kisses all over her face as he wrapped her in his arms.

While she would have normally agreed with everything he said and had waited for the day when he recognized her warrior stature, she knew she didn't want to remember. "I'm not afraid. I'm just . . . Darwu, you don't understand. I don't think I—"

"Kara, you need to open all of yourself to me or else we won't be able to make it. You have been inside me. You know all there is to know. I need the same." His eyes narrowed momentarily and he sighed. "If you are holding anything back, it leaves room for betrayal, I can't say I will be as soft with your lessons as I was today."

Kara sucked her teeth. *Soft! Who are you kidding? If you call that soft then I'd hate to see what you call hard.*

Exactly, you don't want to see. And I don't want to have to show you. So, please, mate, open all of yourself to me. Let me inside. Let me see if I can help you to uncover and remember. Darwu led her over to a bed in the corner of the room.

Besides the various straps and ties attached to the bed, it appeared to be a regular cot with a soft fluffy mattress. As they climbed onto the bed and settled in the middle, she tried to get away from the overwhelming sense of fear and premonition quickly surrounding her.

Her heart pounded in her chest and small trickles of sweat laced her brow. Trying to breathe felt like a task. Closing her eyes, she told herself to calm down, to relax, but she couldn't.

Look at me, Kara.

Opening her eyes and tilting her head upwards, Kara gazed into Darwu's firm, secure stare and suddenly her hands didn't feel so clammy. Her heart rate almost returned to normal and her breathing seemed to take on a nice steady pace.

Darwu had no idea what had Kara in such a state of fear, but he was determined to uncover this mystery. The woman hadn't been truly afraid or heeded any of his warnings since they met. He had to know what from her past frightened her so.

From what he could tell, from her thoughts and the snippets from the discussion with her uncle, she was hiding from herself.

How does one hide from oneself? It was impossible, wasn't it? Surely her uncle was just playing with her mind. But there was that one small space inside of her he couldn't penetrate, even after she had opened her entire self to him. And it appeared as if she barely knew it was there. As though it was a space she'd never visited.

Darwu clasped her hands in his and leaned forward. They sat facing one another on the bed. As he took in her incredible beauty, he knew he had to find a way to free her from whatever she was hiding from herself.

Kara, listen to me. I don't want you to be afraid. I'm here for you. I'm here with you. We will face this together. Your fate is mine and mine is yours. You are the other half of my soul. I need you whole in order to be whole myself. I feel that in the deepest part of me. And I know once we free you, we will both be free. Can you do this for us?

Kara's gaze faltered a little and he thought he was going to lose her. Taking a deep breath, she shook her head. *I will do it for us and for our sons. I hope you are right and this doesn't bring danger to our path. I have this bad feeling it will.*

If it does, we will face it together, Warrior Princess. I don't think I would want any other beside me in battle but my feisty mate. Darwu brushed his lips across hers before deepening his kiss. The soft sweet taste of her felt like nourishment.

When I was inside your mind, heart and soul earlier, I found one space that remained closed to me no matter what I did. I think this is where we need to start. It's in the far recesses of your mind. I'm going back there and I want you to come with me.

No.

Yes. Kara. Yes.

Please no. Can't we just—.

Darwu wrapped his arms around her. *The memory is so far in the back of your mind, it must be from your childhood. I'm thinking it may have something to do with your parents' death and the destruction of your village. I have been having nightmares about that day from your eyes ever since I couldn't save you. I now know there must have been a Divine reason for that. Let me go back with you, Kara so we can face this together. Please.*

Maybe, what I need to know isn't there. How do we know its something from—from then? Maybe I need—.

Kara, don't be afraid. I know you are brave. I've seen it. Darwu touched her face before covering her mouth with a kiss. He didn't know why, but after merging and becoming one with her so intensely, he knew he had to help her. He couldn't stop until she found herself. The nagging feeling in his gut wouldn't allow him to let her continue hiding. Deepening his kiss, he placed an image in her mind of the nightmare he'd had for the past ten years.

At the sight of herself as a little girl, Kara tried to break away from the kiss. He wrapped his arms tightly around her and held her, keeping the physical as well a mental connection. Together they replayed the events and soon she was able to slowly move further back, to before they met as children. What he saw startled him.

"Do you think it's wise to let her go around exhibiting her power so freely," Yuken asked his mate. The tall, unusually pale man leaned back in the wooden chair he'd crafted with leftover stray pieces, and stared at the woman he'd loved since before he even knew what love was.

Sara had studied the Divine prophecies and she'd even dreamed of what would happen to them before she ever met and mated with him. Any other man would have run from the ravishing brown-skinned beauty with copper flashes in her eyes and wild tales in her head. But he couldn't.

Their daughter, Kara, had been having dreams ever since she was five. The only problem was *she* wanted to change everyone's fate.

The entire village contained people who were happy and contented, their every desire realized. They owed it all to a little girl getting stronger and stronger everyday. A ten-year-old who no matter how much happiness, well being and goodness she spread throughout the community, wasn't yet strong enough to stop destiny from taking its course.

He'd thought it odd the first time he saw it happen, but he couldn't deny what he saw with his own eyes. The Rancle family's crop had been declared a failure. They weren't going to be able to pay their taxes and they were going to be kicked off the land. The night he told his wife about the vision he couldn't find Kara anywhere.

Because of who she was and the prophecy, he worried anytime his little girl went missing. Despite her having power he never would truly understand, she was still his little girl.

After searching all over the village he found her kneeling in front of the Rancle's farm. With eyes closed and hands lifted to the great beyond, she chanted a soft prayer-plea to the Divine. She hadn't wanted to leave when he finally pulled her away. He knew she would have stayed all night.

The next morning the Rancle's had a crop. Baffled, he didn't know what she had done. Though her prayers didn't always work, the majority of the time they did.

As he waited for his mate to respond with the answer he knew even before he asked the question, he allowed himself to wish they could find another way.

"I think flexing her mental muscles and using her powers so much is fine. The people in the village are happy." Sara waved her hand dismissively and smiled at her daughter before turning to her husband.

"Yes, but most of them don't know they will soon be dead. I think using her powers is what will bring the unwanted notice. If we could find a way to stop her from using them, to hide them, then maybe we won't all have to die and we can raise our daughter ourselves until she is old enough to fulfill her destiny." Yuken pleaded with Sara the way he had from the time Kara started exhibiting her powers.

Kara watched her parents argue and sighed knowing it was her fault. She almost wished they would just be happy and never have any disagreements.

For some reason, that didn't last long when she wished it for them. She had done so lots of times before, but they always somehow came back to the prophesy, her powers and the fact her entire village was going to die unless she figured out away to save them all.

Most of the time whenever she felt sadness, Kara simply willed happiness in the name of the Divine. Some of the people stayed happy and some continued to be sad. Things like crops and having money to pay the tax collectors seemed a whole lot easier to do than making sure no one was sad.

She would say a prayerful chant and ask the Divine, and crops grew. She blessed homes and protected the entire village with her prayers. The darkness that loomed just outside the village never seemed to fully penetrate it. Sometimes though, when she was sleeping, the darkness seeped into the village. That was when she saw the mean, scary man with the yellow eyes that glowed with evil. The man wanted to hurt her. The man wanted her dead. Even though she managed to remain hidden from him, she didn't know if the Divine was going to help her stop him.

Everyone in the village always had their taxes paid on time and their bellies were full. Kara prayed for it. When the Divine answered she was happy. When the Divine decided not to allow a crop yield or help a family who couldn't come up with all their taxes on their own, Kara learned to be fine with that as well. Her mother told her she had power, but it was still up to the Divine to manifest it. She didn't know if the Divine could make the man with the glowing yellow eyes go away.

Joy flowed freely and Kara wouldn't have it any other way. Once she realized she could bring happiness to the villagers, she did everything within her power to do so. Sometimes she prayed instead of playing with the other children. She prayed the Divine would stop the evil her father said was going to kill them all.

Many times in her dreams, she felt the bad man. She could see him chanting, trying to find her. At first it had been funny watching him get angry when he couldn't find her, almost like hide and seek, but one time in her dreams the bad man hurt another little girl. They cut her badly and used her blood to bring out the most evil being she'd ever seen. That was when she knew they'd be coming to her village soon. She's hoped her father was wrong and she would be able to stop the slaughter. So she made her mother give her more lessons to control her power and make herself stronger. The stronger she became, the stronger the beam of Divine light shined on her village.

She knew she had to become stronger still. Strong enough to keep the crops growing, and strong enough to keep people happy. However, upsetting her father hurt her, and she thought maybe she should not upset him so often.

As soon as Kara made her decision, her mother had come running over to the corner where she prayed.

"Kara, I need you to hurry to the tunnel we set up for you and hide until your uncle Rafe comes for you." Her mother's eyes were wide. Kara could tell she wasn't frightened for herself, but for Kara.

The bad thing was happening. Kara couldn't stop it happening. She wanted her parents to stay with her. "Come with me, momma. Please don't stay here. I can protect you and daddy."

Sara rubbed her hand through Kara's hair as she walked her towards the tunnel. "That's not our destiny, dear one. Our destiny was simply to make you. Now you must go through the tunnel. They are here."

"I can try and stop them," Kara pleaded.

"No, they will find you and kill you like they are killing everyone else. Now go into the tunnel. Run until you can't run any more and don't stop for anyone except Rafe."

Divine Destiny

The screaming and pain came closer and closer to their little home. Kara could feel it all around her and knew her mother was right. She hurried into her closet and opened the secret hatch leading to the underground tunnel her uncle and father had built for her.

Hearing the front door kick in, Sara waved Kara away. "Hurry child, go and know we will always love you."

Kara pretended to leave and was just coming back out of the hatch when she saw the big bad man take an ax and bash it into her mother's head. Her mouth flew open but no sound came out. Her father tried to wrestle the ax away from the man. Before she could react, or call upon the Divine, she watched in horror as another soldier thrust a sword into her father's belly. Her father just stood there for a moment. To Kara, he looked as if he were staring right at her, as his eyes grew dim and the light that had always been bright as daylight to her, faded to nothing.

She could feel the men's brutality. What was the use of having the stupid Divine power if she couldn't do something to bring her parents back? She was only a little girl. She needed her mommy and daddy.

"Divine, hide me, cloak me, save me. Hide me. Cloak me. Save me." Kara mumbled as she tip-toed out of the room. Hadn't her mother always said she had the power to make the Divine will be done? She could do it. She could protect herself and she could bring her parents back.

Believing herself invisible, Kara came out of her bedroom just as the king's army was leaving. Why would the king kill her parents? Why would he have his army murder an entire village?

Her father's words from his many arguments with her mother came back to her as she stared down at his now lifeless, bloody body. Using her powers had brought the danger to everyone.

Kneeling down in the pool of blood between her two beautiful parents, she decided then and there she would never use her power again. Kara touched her mother's face and then her father's hand.

She couldn't bring herself to look into his lightless eyes. She almost willed them to live. Could she make one last use of her power to bring them back?

"Are we sure we killed the girl?" An angry voice asked from close outside their home.

"The Cultide is not sensing her power anymore. She must be one of the little girls we killed." Another male voice added.

Kara gasped and tears trailed down her face.

"Then we can stop killing and leave this place?" The first man asked.

"No, the king wants the entire village dead. The homes burned and the ground scorched. He was firm, no more potential shamanesses should come from this village. They are getting stronger and stronger and can't be properly corrupted." Their footsteps seemed as though they were coming back toward the house. Their voices seemed to be getting closer.

She should have listened to her mother. Kara quickly jumped up and ran to her tunnel.

Once in the underground tunnel, she ran as fast as her feet could carry her until the tunnel ended. She thought about staying there until her uncle came, like her mother told her, but she sensed that there was help nearby, so she exited the tunnel and ran directly into an boy.

Kara opened her eyes and gazed into the eyes of her mate. He'd come to save her then and he was trying to save her now. Would he still want to save her knowing what she was, knowing her parents died because of her. That her entire village had died because of her?

"I will love you and remain by your side for the rest of our lives. You never have to worry about me not being there for you. And you didn't kill your parents." Darwu paused before continuing angrily.

"I can't believe my father would do this. You were my mate. How could he try to kill you and all of those people?"

"Because of who I am. I shouldn't have been using my powers. Then he wouldn't have known." Tears fell from her eyes like a waterfall. The guilt she felt threatened to overtake her and all she wanted to do was run and never stop.

No. Darwu grasped her shoulders and gazed lovingly into her eyes. She didn't see any blame there, only love.

"You need to tap into your power, Kara. You've cloaked it somehow and hidden it from yourself. You need to undo what you did."

Shaking her head vehemently, Kara tried to remove herself from Darwu's arms. "No. The king will kill us both. I can't let them kill you, Darwu. I couldn't bear it if you also died because of me. My uncle is going to be killed. My parents are dead. And it's all my fault."

"It's not your fault. The castle is corrupt. Maybe if you can find your strength and power, you can bring the joy and happiness like you did in the village."

Kara shook her head no and tried to get up from the bed. Darwu held her and pulled her close. He placed his lips over hers and kissed her. Allowing himself to fully merge with her again, mind, body, and soul, he smiled.

I know now you poured love over me, washing away my concerns giving me a sense of peace in these past couple of days. As soon as I felt sadness, you acted. That was your power. That was what caused the glow. You have to do it to yourself, but I'll help.

Totally submerged, Kara could barely distinguish her thoughts from Dawru's, her acts from his. She could feel him, could feel his hands on her, feel her hands on him. Ripples of love and sensations. Bubbles of joy and peace.

Let's think about the happiness our hearts have been yearning for since we met again. Fighting over the silliest things when we should have been connecting and loving one another. We can see together what was impossible to see apart. Freedom should always reign. Free yourself, Kara so we can free others.

A bright beam of gold began to eek its way from inside her and started to cover them both. With each burst of golden light, shimmers and sparks surrounded them. Soon a bright aura surrounded them both and Kara felt her heart opening up and pouring out into the room.

Looking around her eyes got wider and wider. The dark sex dungeon glowed. She felt her strength and spoke.

"Divine will be done. Uncloak me. Give me the power I ran away from. Allow me to be again who the Divine one meant me to be. I won't hide from my responsibility or my fate. I will do what needs to be done so that freedom reigns and all people are allowed their true destinies."

Kara closed her eyes and went deep inside herself. She found it then. All the things her mother had taught her and all the things she'd learned on her own. She'd outgrown her mother's training early for a young shamaness.

She wondered if she would ever truly get back all she'd forsaken. When she opened her eyes, Dawru was still holding her, a bronze glimmer cloaking him. She looked down at her hands and saw a copper haze.

"We're both different. Whatever you uncloaked in you also untapped something deep in me. I have never felt this kind of power—I suppose that's what it is—before." Darwu studied his bronze glimmer with awe.

Kara took a deep breath and centered herself. The difference in Darwu was greater than he realized. She had no idea she was mated to such a powerful man. Everything she'd seen in him when she had first entered his mind and soul was amplified. His warrior strength, cunning skill, and stellar mind were now tempered with and fortified by love and purpose.

Touching his face, she smiled. "You have everything you need now to rule Ourlane, fairly."

"To co-rule. I know this deep inside now. The King's Divine Shamaness is his co-ruler." Darwu pulled her closer and brushed his lips across hers. "The corruption that has been allowed to reign, allowed men to rule with the advice of a council of other power-hungry men. The shamanesses in the past were stripped of their Divine power and corrupted. Years of this caused the pain to pulse through the land."

"What are we going to do?" Kara didn't know if they could really take on an entire corrupt castle by themselves.

"I'm going to put an end to this and then we will rule together." Darwu seemed to forget the co-rule thing as soon as he said it and it irritated Kara to no end.

"*You're* going to put an end to this? You mean you intend to go up against the throne by yourself, even though as you have just stated, we are meant to co-rule? We are one, Darwu. We're meant to face this battle together."

"You're carrying my sons. This could be dangerous. I won't hear any arguments on this, Kara. We can strategize together but we will not fight together, not while you are with child." The adamant finality in his voice made her cringe.

Kara rolled her eyes and let out a huff of breath. Even after all he'd seen, he'd learned nothing. By all that was Divine, when would that change? Would it ever?

"Divine will be done, Darwu. I know what that truly means now. We can't stop doing what is good and righteous because we are afraid of losing something. We have to always strive to do the right thing, even if we lose our lives, because in doing so, we are insuring that Divine will and goodness will eventually reign. I want to do my part. And I won't be denied that right." Removing herself from his grasp, she folded her arms across her chest.

Darwu crossed his own arms and gave her a pointed stare. "Either you will do this my way, or I will tie you up and lock you down here until I'm done."

Anger heated her face and she forced herself not to leap onto Darwu massive shoulders and pummel his thick head with her fists. "Fine. But we will strategize this first together. Then we will free my uncle and the others."

"Fine. Your uncle and the other reb—freedom fighters will be released."

"So, if the Cultide and not the Divine has been the power behind the throne for so long, who do we go after? The culprit has to be someone who is close to the king and advisor to the throne."

"That would have to be my Uncle Alto."

"Or your mother." Kara knew something was odd about the queen.

"My mother! How can you think such a thing? And anyway, the Cultide is so entrenched it would have been in place long before my mother ever came to the castle." Darwu wouldn't hear anything bad about his mother.

Kara tried to decide if her problems with the queen had more to do with her determination to see Kara in a dress. "Okay, so maybe it's not your mother, but she is corrupt."

"They are all corrupted. That's what the Cultide power does. How do we cut out the root of its power in a way that frees those corrupted by it? We need to save them." Darwu appeared to think his family could be saved.

While Kara wasn't exactly sure about that, she knew she had to try for his sake. "We can try. I'm thinking if we find the Cultide priest or priestess, we will find the root of its power."

"Then I will start with Uncle Alto. It's time to get dressed and end this once and for all."

Once dressed, they left the sexual torture chamber and went to the cells. As soon as they approached the cell that housed her uncle and the others, Kara noticed a marked difference in her uncle's demeanor.

"Well, men take a look at what Ourlane hasn't seen for ages. A divinely matched royal couple uncorrupted and set to co-rule for the good of the land. I see you have found yourself, niece." Rafe actually smiled at her and Darwu.

The men all went to their knees and bowed including Rafe. Kara couldn't believe what she was witnessing. Apparently neither could Darwu.

"I don't think I ever seen members of The Resistance give reverence to royals before." Stunned, Darwu stopped in mid-step.

"We have never had an uncorrupted royalty to pay reverence to, Your Highness. Can't you feel it? The entire aura of the castle has changed now that the two of you have tapped into your Divine power? You needed each other to do it and Divine will can now be done." Rafe slowly rose, still keeping his head bowed respectfully.

"What are you some kind of prophet or something?" Darwu asked incredulously.

Rafe shook his head and smiled. "No, Your Highness. I interpret Divine prophecies and play my role in aiding Divine will, but I'm not a prophet."

"Well, since we now know The Resistance wasn't responsible for the murder and destruction, but instead the king's army, we are going to let you go. You need to know the current throne still sees The Resistance as traitors and until we are able to reverse the corruption, your lives will still be in jeopardy." Dawru unlocked the cell and opened it.

Rafe and the other men exited the cell. Kara couldn't help but roll her eyes and hiss in disgust.

I'm sure your uncle has his reasons for not allowing you to free them earlier.

Kara knew her uncle had good reasons and she was glad he hadn't allowed her to rescue him and the others. Rafe touched her face and lifted her chin. He smiled at her and she smiled back in understanding.

"We are going to show you the way out of the castle where you can be certain to escape undetected—"

Rafe interrupted Darwu, "If it's all the same, Your Highness, we would like to stay and help you in any way we can. You will need our help to flush out the source of the corruption. Also, my mate is here in the castle and I won't be leaving without her."

"You have a mate in the castle? But of course, how else would The Resistance have the information they seemed to be able to acquire with very little effort." It became clear Darwu didn't know exactly how he was supposed to feel about that piece of information.

Kara smiled because it suddenly struck her who her uncle's mate had to be. "Donia," she said more to herself than to anyone else.

"Yes, Kara. How did you know?" Rafe's face lit up and it was clear he was thinking about his mate.

"Just a lucky guess, really. She's one of the few people in the castle who hasn't given me the creeps and I felt like I could trust her from the first moment I met her." Happy her warrior senses were still intact, and she could tell friend from foe, Kara let out a sigh.

"Well, much as I would like to stand here and find out what other spies The Resistance had in the castle, we need to hurry and get started flushing out the source of the corruption. If you all want to help, that will be great. That way we can keep Kara out of harm's way." Darwu started walking away and Kara followed behind him.

"I don't think that is a good idea," Kara snapped. "We need to do this together. We are stronger together than we are apart."

"She's right," Rafe said, "but the two of you are connected and therefore you are never apart. What's his is yours and what's yours is his. So, if you can keep yourself out of immediate danger and let your mate handle it, why not?"

Rafe seemed to have all the answers. And while she at one time would have followed her uncle anywhere and listened to his every command, Kara found herself detesting his current line of thought and action.

How can a freedom fighter have such a dated, antiquated approach to things, Kara wondered as she stared at her uncle incredulously. Had he always been that way?

Fuming didn't even begin to describe her state of mind. Near explosive seemed a more apt description. Did they not realize she was a warrior, too? Did she not fight side by side with her uncle and the others in the bush? She even led battles against the corrupt monarchy.

Was she or was she not a shamaness? Granted, she had just started to come into power, but Darwu had no more or less experience than she did in that regard. Just thinking about it made her angrier.

Don't be upset, Kara. No one is questioning your battle skills or your ability to handle yourself. I'd just feel better if we played it a little safe, with the future heirs to the throne inside of you. Darwu wrapped a protective arm around her and she shrugged it off as she walked ahead of him and the other men.

Oh and of course it's all about making you feel better. Stopping in front of the cell that held Gab and the soldier she stopped. "What about these two?"

Darwu's face took on a harsh angry glare as he surveyed his cousin.

Gab leaned against the cell with a sick and twisted snarl on his face. "Well I never thought I'd see the day when Darwu, the Warrior Prince, would commit such a treasonous act against the throne. Freeing The Resistance. Is the sex that good, cousin?"

Darwu leaped toward the cell angrily reaching to open it before Rafe stopped him.

"He's not worth it. We need to carry on, Your Highness." Rafe held a firm grasp on Dawru's arm.

Clutching the bars of the cell, Darwu hissed, "I will be back to take care of you, cousin. You put your hands on my mate! Mark my words, you will suffer the penalty for that. You and your brother."

Rafe pulled him away as Kara stood in front of the cell.

"By all that is Divine, Gab, it would be nice if the evil inside of you just ate its way through and took care of you once and for all." Kara calmly spoke the words she was feeling and turned to walk away.

Rafe turned around with a startled expression. "Kara, you have to be careful with your words." His eyes widened as he stared into the cell.

Darwu and the men took on horrified expressions causing Kara to turn back towards the cell.

Gab lay on the floor writhing with curds of black slime foaming from his mouth. He started convulsing and shaking, his body rising several inches from the ground before falling back to the floor with a bam. He did this for several minutes until he simply stopped moving and remained in the pool of the black filth that seemed to seep from every orifice and pore of his body.

Kara covered her mouth and turned away. The dungeon began to smell like rotten food. The smell wafted around them, the aura thick and dark. The clouds of dark-red evil bounced around the dungeon. It shimmied over the walls and seemed to want to penetrate each and every one of them. She watched as it circled all of them, even the soldier still locked in the cell with the now dead Gab. The red haze concentrated itself and barreled at the soldier, but still remained outside. Each defeated push made the air thicker until the evil putrid haze wafted up the stairway and away from them all.

Darwu stared at her as if she had two heads. Even her comrades gazed at her uneasily. The only person who didn't seem perturbed by her apparent ability to kill a man by just invoking the name of the Divine was her Uncle Rafe.

"Kara, what was the first thing your mother taught you when you were a young girl, just coming into your powers?" The matter-of-fact, dry tone of Rafe's voice gave her pause.

How was she supposed to remember the first thing her mother taught her?

And then, just as clearly as anything, she remembered the mean dog that used to chase her when she played outside alone. The dog had actually bitten one of her friends. She'd wished the evil dog gone. Just before she wished him dead though, his eyes glowed yellow and he seemed almost possessed. The dog had dropped dead and her neighbor came to complain. That was when her mother decided it would be better to start her training early and help her control her powers.

Kara, your words have more strength than the average person, especially when you call on the Divine. You have to be careful what you say and how you say it. Those had been her mother's words.

"I'm sorry. I really didn't mean for him to die. But he was just so full of evil. Didn't you all see it circling us looking for a new place to nest and corrupt?" Kara defended herself as best she could. The last thing she wanted was for her mate and her comrades to be afraid of her.

"Yes, we saw it." Darwu finally spoke and she felt a calm overcome her. She could tell by his tone of voice he didn't think she was odd or abnormal, but he had been a little taken aback by the way Gab had died. "It's not your fault. The evil inside of him long ago killed anything good about him before you spoke those words. I only hope we can save the others."

"Excuse me, Your Highness." The soldier inside the cell held his nose as he spoke and stood as far away from Gab's putrid body as he could get. "Please don't leave me in here with this dead body. I have served under you and served you well. And I would gladly follow you in any battle. I am truly sorry for putting my hands on your mate. But at the time I thought she had no business down here and I was simply trying to bring her back to you."

"And she gave you a nice beating for your trouble, didn't she?" Nic offered with a laugh. Clearly he'd seen the fight between Kara and the soldier and had gotten a kick out of it.

"I only tried to restrain her, not harm her. I would never think to harm your mate, Sir. Please." The soldier took to begging.

Kara felt sorry for the soldier. After studying him carefully she realized he truly would stand by Darwu in any battle. And she had a feeling that they would need all the help they could get going up against the king and the others.

Unlike Darwu, she harbored little hope that any of them could be saved, but she was willing to try. They were his parents after all, and she would give anything to have her mother and father with her again.

Darwu placed his arms around her. It felt good to know that he would always know when she needed comfort and would give it as often as he could.

"I think you can trust him, Darwu. But he's your soldier and you know that. You may need his help to do what you hope to do." Kara offered.

Darwu opened the cell and let the soldier out. The man embraced Darwu and couldn't stop thanking him.

Kara decided then and there if Darwu really didn't want her to fight in the battle with him and the others, she would respect his wishes. She'd respect them, but she didn't have to like it.

Chapter 15

The aura of the entire castle shifted. The altar to the Cultide collapsed onto itself just after the last of the candles flickered out.

The king stood in the secret Cultide worship and ritual room taking in the site with considerable apprehension. The change could only mean one thing: the girl was no longer hiding her powers and she had somehow gotten to Darwu.

The light and airy feeling along with the bright and blooming turn signaled a Divinely matched royal pair. Not only was his son now mated with *the one*, but she also brought him fully into himself before they were able to corrupt him.

He could no longer save Darwu now. The situation had turned into kill or be killed.

"No. Never!"

The king turned. He hadn't even noticed his wife coming into the hidden sanctuary.

"Hietha—" The king tried to placate his mate. Surely she had to see Darwu presented a threat to all they knew and held dear. The son and his mate now posed a threat to their very lives.

"I won't let you just kill my son. He's all I have. He's my only child. Your corruption spoiled me and I couldn't bear any more fruit. I won't let you take Darwu from me." Heitha's harsh words hit their mark.

His wife's devotion to their son had always pained him. As his mate, she was supposed to take his side over anyone, including their own child if need be.

In an attempt to get her to see the error of her ways and stop herself before she said something they would both regret, the king spoke softly and soothingly in his mate's mind. *Hietha, darling, please understand* —

"Get out of my head. As long as you harbor ill thoughts against my child — our son — our only son, you are no longer welcomed. Now I am going to go and warn him — "

Before his beloved mate could walk out the door he struck her with the metal candelabra. Had she not closed her mind to him she might have seen it coming. Instead, his mate now lay dying on the floor, a stream of blood running and congealing at the back of her head.

Without his queen, the only thing he had left was the throne, and he wasn't about to let anyone take it from him, not even his son.

Although she wasn't particularly happy about being left in the suite for safekeeping, Kara tried to maintain good spirits. Even after they saw what she could do just by speaking and deeming Divine will, they still managed to make a case for keeping her away from the action. She sat alone in their quarters while Darwu and the men she'd fought side by side with them for years to bring downa corrupt monarchy went to finish the job. Where was the fairness in that?

The longer she sat, the more she realized she needed to be at Darwu's side. The only problem was now that he had fully merged with her and broken through all her defenses she had no way of doing anything without him knowing.

They were closer and more connected; and she could see the serious downside of their bond.

Her warrior mate still had a lot to learn about equality. The years were certainly going to be interesting if he didn't change his ways.

Startled by the slamming of the door, Kara looked up expecting to see Darwu. Instead she saw the king and Prince Alto. She didn't need her heightened awareness to let her know things were about to get hectic. She discerned the malicious looks on the two men's faces without tapping into her special powers.

"Well, do you mean to tell me I've been here all this time and I finally get my welcome and personal audience with the king?" She spoke the words in a dry disinterested voice even as her heart had started to palpitate rapidly.

"You'd be wise to tame your tongue. If you do then perhaps we will make your death quick and painless." The king's eyes widened and he appeared a bit crazed.

"Since I don't plan on dying today, you might want to think about your own tongue. In fact, you might want to think about using it to pray I take mercy on you and let you live to find redemption." Kara stood and walked toward the other side of the room, away from the two men.

Dawru, your father and Uncle are here and I don't want a repeat of what happened to your cousin. But, well, you understand I'm not going to let them harm me, not with the babies to consider. Even though she believed the entire lot of Darwu's relatives were truly beyond repair, she wanted to give her mate the chance to try and help them.

If the string of curses ringing out from Darwu in her mind were indication, he seemed genuinely peeved he hadn't been able to keep her from the action.

An evil grin crossed the king's face. "Are you communicating with my son? If you are, you can tell him to come. By the time he gets here, you will be dead and then we can kill him since you have already made him useless to the Cultide."

"You would kill your own son just to ensure the continued corrupt rule of the Cultide?" Shocked, Kara could hardly believe what she heard. Sure, she knew the king had threatened them both. She figured if it came down to it, they would kill her and let Darwu live.

Taking a deep breath she smiled as brightly and as falsely as she ever had. "Well surely you realize I can't let you kill my mate. So, why don't the two of you just do yourselves a favor and get out of the castle, hell, get out of the Providence of Ourlane before this gets ugly."

"It's a little too late for escape, you silly girl. You have set a course in motion that can only end two ways: with us dead, or you and Darwu dead. You really should have stayed wherever you were. Now you will have to pay the ultimate price: your life." Prince Alto took menacing steps toward her and she almost laughed. Did the fat prince really hope to cause her harm?

"Now that I have found my mate, I have too much to live for. I'm not really in the mood to die today. I do think, however, that you should join your son Gab. The evil that rotted him from inside out is in you. By all that is Divine let the evil rot its way out of you and end the miserable existence you call a life." This time Kara watched closely as Alto lurched and the evil gunk purged from his body leaving him a pathetic writhing mess on the floor. This time the red haze and muck didn't circulate for long. It went directly into the king.

"So you are as powerful as they say. But you are not as powerful as you need to be to beat a Cultide king such as myself." The king barely spared his brother a glance as he studied Kara. His eyes glowed yellow and he took on a possessed and crazed appearance.

She realized she hadn't been seeing things the times she observed the change in his eye color. More importantly, she recognized him as the evil man from her childhood dreams. The one, who had been determined to find her, the one so determined to have her gone, he sent an army to destroy an entire village. The need for revenge took over, and Kara found herself wanting to make the king pay for the damage and pain he'd caused everyone.

"I don't know, *Your Highness*. But I guess you're determined for us to find out. I'd hate to have to turn you into a puddle of black puss and goo like Alto and Gab. But if you force me, then I will."

The king laughed and started walking towards her. She refused to show fear, so she stood her ground even when he was right in front of her. The huge bulking masculine presence might have scared a lesser woman, but not her.

Perhaps her newfound powers had made her a little too self-assured. Because, no sooner had she finished thinking she wasn't afraid, when the king grab her hair and tried to pull her close. Struggling with everything she had, Kara could only manage to kick the large king in the shin, even though she'd been aiming much higher.

His eyes narrowed as he snatched her forward with seemingly no effort. His strength appeared unnatural. Then she realized all the evil that had been split amongst the royals, had found a resting spot in the king.

Pulling her by the hair, the king reached a hand toward her stomach. She tried to wiggle out of his grasp and was even willing to lose the patch of her hair, but the king's strength proved too great.

He placed his hand on her stomach and spoke in a hushed halting voice. "And I would hate to stand here while you bleed out the beginnings of the two in your womb who share my genes. We both know they can't be allowed to live and neither can you. I call on the darkness of the Cultide to yank the life growing in your womb so that the blood of my blood goes back to darkness where it belongs!"

The king removed his hand and Kara felt a sharp shooting pain lace her womb. Grabbing her stomach as she toppled over, she fought with everything inside of her to hold on to her sons. The combination of the pain and all of the energy she directed toward the Divine willing it to save her babies incapacitated her.

Picking her up as if she weighed nothing and stepping over Alto's lifeless body, the king walked and offered threats as he did so. "My son will be here soon and since I'm not quite done with you and no longer have Alto to help me—thanks to you—I think its best we find another place to finish you off. It's a shame really. You are a pretty little thing. Maybe, I'll have a little fun with you before I'm done."

Kara held onto the small pulps of life that were to be her children even as the evil seemed to claw at her guts. Calling on the Divine didn't seem to be helping, so she reached for Darwu with a small bit of her energy and almost felt one of the babies drop.

Tsking, the king gave her a shaking jolt as he carried her off. "You might as well let them die. They are going to die anyway and so are you." The king carried her through his chambers and touched the back wall behind his desk. The wall opened and they entered into a semi dark room that appeared to be some sort of ritual center.

Kara noticed that he had stepped over the body of the queen as soon as he threw her down next to the woman. Hitting the floor with a thud, Kara winced. It was getting harder and harder to hold the babies. She began to resign herself to losing the children she hadn't thought she wanted. The sadness overcoming her felt like another life force and quickly began to take her breath away.

As Kara struggled to breath and hold the children inside, she looked at the woman lying next to her. The queen was breathing with great difficulty.

Queen Heitha reached out her hand and touched Kara's belly. It angered Kara that she didn't have the energy to pull away. The queen would probably try to finish what the king started and kill her babies.

A tear fell down Kara's face and the queen smiled. The brightness that came from the older woman at that moment shook Kara to her core. Kara had never seen so much goodness and light radiating from the queen. As quickly as it appeared the pain stopped. And the queen died.

"I know you're not going to want to hear this, but we may need to think about finding a way to lend Kara your strength so that she can fight them." Rafe pulled Darwu to the side as they searched the castle looking for the king and Kara. "We don't have a lot of time. She is strong but I don't think she can go up against your father. He has been corrupted by the Cultide for too long. She'll need your strength just as you would have needed hers."

Darwu glared at Kara's uncle. He could tell by the sudden faint pleading, that Kara was indeed in trouble. When they stormed into the suite only to find Alto's rotting body and no Kara, Darwu didn't know what to think or where to look.

They combed every inch of the castle and couldn't find his mother, father or Kara. He didn't want to believe his parents would harm his mate. Now it seemed as if he had no choice. He did know he would kill anyone who touched her.

"What should we do then, Rafe? I'm not going to stop looking for her. We have to find her." Darwu had never felt so helpless and he didn't want to ever feel that way again.

"She needs your strength right now to defeat your father. You won't be able to go to her physically and get there in time. You need to merge with her mentally. You have to give all of yourself to her now before it's too late." Rafe spoke as if he knew what he was talking about, but still Darwu wondered how such a thing could be done.

The only time he and Kara had fully merged had been earlier that day when he was helping her recover herself. Would he even be able to do the same thing when he didn't have a clue where she was? Did he even have a choice right now? "Fine, what can I do to help her? Just tell me what to do."

"You have to die," Rafe offered in a matter-of-fact tone.

"What!" Taking a step back, Darwu readied himself for attack. He should have known better that to trust The Resistance. Why hadn't he known better?

"You won't be totally dead." Rafe seemed to sense his distrust and smiled assuredly. "But you will be in a deep enough sleep so that your mind can find hers and merge. You won't have a lot of time, so you will have to find her, get in there, merge and destroy the king fairly quickly. You can't sleep the sleep of the dead for an overly extended time. If you stay under too long, then you run the risk of not being able to return."

He knew he would do whatever was needed to save Kara. His heart wouldn't allow for anything else.

Chapter 16

Kara couldn't believe the queen was actually dead. Even though she hadn't liked the woman, she would have never wished her dead. And judging from the way the king was pacing, ranting and raving around the room, he knew his mate was gone as well.

"It's all your fault. I should have gone to that village and killed you myself, instead of sending my brother and my army to destroy your village. Now my mate is gone and I am going to have to destroy the only thing I have left of her, the son she adored, because you've ruined him."

Staying as still as she could, Kara decided not to anger the king further. Since Darwu and the others hadn't found her yet, she figured soon the king would carry out his threat.

Reaching for Darwu one more time with her mind, she was surprised when she suddenly felt his presence more strongly than she ever had. She felt it more strongly than she'd felt it when they had merged together during their most intimate moment.

Darwu?

I'm with you. How are you? The babies?

I'm fine. Although your father is about to kill me. The babies are fine. Thanks to your mother. She spent the last of her energy and power saving them. She had some good in her, Darwu. She could have been a strong shamaness had she mated with the right person. Closing her eyes and willing herself not to cry, because warriors didn't cry, Kara paused.

How did she tell her mate she was afraid and she didn't want to die? She'd faced many battles, but battling the king was huge. She'd already seen what he could do just by calling on the Cultide. He'd almost killed her babies, almost ripped them from her womb with words. She shuddered.

I know everything you're feeling and it's going to be fine. I'm with you now. You will need to use my strength and your own to defeat him. And we don't have a lot of time. You need to get up—What in all that is Divine! Dawru's shocked words came as soon as the king's foot kicked Kara. She could only assume that since Darwu was merged with her, he felt the kicks too. He must have also felt the king pulling her up from the ground by her hair.

In all the battles she had gone through throughout her life, she had never felt more fear. She wasn't going to be able to fight him. She wouldn't win. How could she, when she was so paralyzed?

The anger in Darwu couldn't be contained. It wouldn't be. She could feel his anger coursing its way through her. Her eyes gazed up at the king against her volition. Darwu clearly controlled her movements now.

Dawru, please don't anger him. All he did was touch my stomach and mumble some words and I almost lost the boys. If it hadn't been for your mother, I would have. I can't—

"By all that is Divine, you have sacrificed the lives and well-being of the people of Ourlane for too long. You have corrupted a woman who was meant to be good and pure and sent to help you lead the people of Ourlane to righteousness, peace and freedom. The evil inside you is great, and the harm you've done with it is even greater. The evil should eat its way out of you, taking your essence and your soul with it, so that you may forever wallow in the corruption you helped to create." Dawru started the chant using her mouth. However, soon they were speaking as one.

Through her eyes, they both watched as the king struggled to maintain himself, watched as he let go of her hair and tumbled to the ground. The glowing yellow eyes faded. The evil that began to bubble out of him thickened in the room as it released and she couldn't breathe. Falling to the ground as she coughed, she didn't see what happened when the King of Ourlane took his last breath.

But she felt it. The evil clawed at her, searching for a home. She prayed her children were safe from it, that they didn't harbor the trait the Cultide found so easily and readily corruptible.

Get up, Kara! You need to get out of here.

Her body lifted from the ground against her will and she felt herself moving toward the door and up the hall until she reached the king's chamber. The ritual chamber imploded on itself. Her feet took on a life of their own and she ran faster than she ever had. She knew the speed was Darwu and she thanked the Divine for the first time ever for giving her to him as a mate.

She didn't stop until she came to a small room and what she saw broke her heart. Her uncle, Donia and the others were standing over Darwu's lifeless body, and strangely, she could no longer feel him with her at all.

Darwu?

Her mental call met with silence and her heart started to race.

Darwu? Again nothing.

She raced over to the table where his still body lay. "Darwu!" Her hand reached for him as she placed her head on his heart. Tears filled her eyes and she looked to her uncle and his mate for answers. "He was just with me, but now he's gone. Uncle Rafe, why isn't he answering me?"

"He's in a deep sleep. He's been under for a while. It was the only way he could give you the strength you needed to defeat the king," Rafe replied.

"Why isn't he waking up?" Irritated that her Uncle couldn't provide her with any answers and appeared just as confused as she, Kara closed her eyes tightly and buried her head in Darwu's chest.

She couldn't lose him. Calling out to the Divine with everything inside of her she willed him to live. She set forth the decree and held him close.

Dawru, you can't leave me now, especially now that I've decided to get used to your bossy controlling ways. Tears flowed freely from her eyes, but she didn't care. If her tears could bring him back she would gladly cry in front of the world, warrior or not.

"I think you're pushing it with that one, my love. We both know you'd rather be burned at the stake than let the world see you crying and risk anyone thinking you less of a warrior." Darwu coughed as he spoke and wrapped his arms around Kara, holding her close. He brought her tearstained face to his and kissed her gently. *I'm okay. We're going to be okay. You're the other half of me and I will never leave you.*

"The king is dead! Long live the king. The queen is dead. Long live the queen." Those words provided the backdrop as the first Divinely matched king and queen embraced and prepared to rule Ourlane together.

Group Discussion Questions:

1. Kara struggles throughout with maintaining her identity as a warrior, fighting for the people, and the growing closeness she feels for Prince Darwu. Do you think she was right to continue to think of the people when it meant going against her Divine mate? Or, do you think that she didn't think of the people enough and gave in to her desire for Darwu too quickly?

2. Darwu lived his life, from the time he thought Kara had died, waiting for the moment he would avenge her death. He intensified the war with The Resistance once he was old enough to go out into battle. Do you think he should have been more open to forgiving The Resistance once he found out that Kara was indeed alive?

3. Influenced by how he had been raised to think about Divine mates, Darwu expects automatic obedience from Kara. He uses several erotic lessons, from spankings to delayed sexual gratification, to get Kara to submit and obey. What did you think of Darwu's attempts at taming Kara?

4. It takes Darwu quite some time to come to see Kara as a warrior. He laughs at the very idea of a Warrior Princess, even though he considers himself a Warrior Prince. When he finally acknowledges his mate as a warrior, do you think it is sincere? Or, will she have to remind him a few times that she is a warrior too?

5. A major theme of Divine Destiny is the idea of equality between partners, in this case between Divine mates; that one was not meant to rule the other but that they must learn to co-rule. What do you think about Darwu and Kara's struggles to get to a place where they could truly value one another and not try and force their wills on one another? Do you think that they may have to revisit the issue of equality in their relationship a few more times before it sticks?

6. What do you think about the side love stories of Rafe and Donia? King Milo and Queen Hietha? How do these two very different ways of being Divine mates enhance the struggles that Darwu and Kara go through?

7. Divine Destiny plays with the fantasy that there is one person out there for everyone; that these relationships connect two parts of the same whole, soul mates. What do you think about the idea of soul mates?

8. The ongoing battle between the Divine and the Cultide is the age-old battle between good and evil. Even though Kara and Darwu are successful at running evil from the castle and bring co-rule back to the land, the Cultide is still out there. Do you think the new King and Queen will remain successful in their battle against evil?

About the Author

Gwyneth Bolton was born and raised in Paterson, New Jersey. She currently lives in Syracuse, New York with her husband, Cedric Bolton. When she was twelve years old, she became an avid reader of romance by sneaking her mother's stash of novels. In the nineties, she was introduced to African-American and multicultural romance novels, and her life hasn't been the same since. While she had always been a reader of romance, she didn't feel inspired to write them until the genre opened up to include other voices. And even then, it took finishing graduate school, several non-fiction publications, and a six-week course at the Loft Literary Center titled "Writing the Romance Novel" before she gathered the courage to start writing her first romance novel. She has a BA and an MA in creative writing and a Ph.D. in English. She teaches classes in writing and women's studies at the college level. When she is not working on her own African-American romance novels, she is curled up with a cup of herbal tea, a warm quilt, and a good book. She welcomes response from readers. Please feel free to write her at P.O. Box 9388 Carousel CTR, Syracuse, New York 13290-9381. You can also e-mail her at gwynethbolton@prodigy.net. Or feel free to visit her website at **http://www.gwynethbolton.com**. *Divine Destiny* is the first installment in her "Sex, Love and Revolution" trilogy.